DECAPITATED GODDESS

500 BC

BY AUTHOR

SYEDA RUQIA ZAIDI

S.R.Z Presents first edition January 2019

DECAPITATED GODDESS

Acknowledgement

First and Foremost, I would like to thank the almighty God for giving me strength to undertake this book. Without his blessings, this achievement would not have been possible.

I want to thank everyone who helped me in writing this book, also for those who never wanted me to give a try.

I would like to appreciate my dear friends and colleagues for their comments and support.

I would like to thank my grandmother Late: Nargis Zaidi whose writing instincts fascinated me towards writing and my grandfather Late: Syed Abbas Raza Zaidi an honorable Judge, who was known for his justice oriented attitude, made me a better decision maker.

I would like to dedicate this book to my Father Late: Syed Ali Abul Hasan Zaidi, my very near and dear father like Late: Mohammed Farooq and who always encouraged me to pen down.

Special thanks to my family and Uncle Mr. Hussain Yamani.

And, of course, most of all, I want to thank someone who is very close to my heart.

SYEDA RUQIA ZAIDI

AUTHOR'S PROFILE

Syeda Ruqia Zaidi was born in India with Arabic roots and a master's degree from a renowned university called "Osmania University" from the "State of Nizam" which is currently called "Hyderabad" and has the inborn desire and admiration in the History running in her veins with lot of positivity in her attitude with her experience in various streams like News Producer, Financial Advisor, Journalism, News Presenter, Special Story writer into different aspects of life. After a Vast experience into her personal and professional life which made her more moderate and conventional to pen down Historical, Fiction, Documentaries , Poetry, Drama, Mystery, Horror, Romance, Anthologies to name a few..

SYEDA RUQIA ZAIDI

Contents

SYNOPSIS

The story is based on a Historical Fiction which makes you tremendously involved in it, which has interesting adventurous magical action packed at one place. Story Follows and revolves around 500 B.C.

During this period everything used to run in and around magic running through veins of every humans whether mortals or immortals. Magic was the common source to connect different worlds through various means. One wrong move or a wrong decision can change the whole world upside down.

The four great emperors fight to save the love of (Paladin) Shamwill from the God of elements who turns out to be barbarous creature who is not only harmful to the love life of Shamwill (Fourth Emperor) but also his evil existence can bring destruction to mankind. They fight with everything including their mystical powers to safeguard the mankind from the brutal and demonic wrath of the God of Elements.

The (Paladin) Shamwill who has a secretive identity in the story is madly in love with the goddess (Amunet), who is exceptionally beautiful externally and internally. The Paladin can stake everything to get her but never wants mankind to be affected. He is left with no choice except a great war to be marked upon the history of living. Struggling with all possible resources and ready to fight. Acquainted with the most updated skills and confident enough about getting back his love from the wrath of evil. Fighting with all uncertainties he takes up a journey to get back his love. Trotting towards the mission to her rescue from evil God for which makes him travel miles and gets through unbelievable mystical obstacles. With all support from the great kings and emperors, he succeeds in getting back the goddess Amunet and declares an epic war against the evil God with rarity.

Story revolves around various adventures and characters, with different deadly weapons which support Shamwill including various Gods with massive powers. The inciting incidents which were going to happen to Shamwill change his whole life when he fell in love with decapitated goddess Amunet. After the mystery is revealed he assures her to fight against evil. The destructive problem arises when he comes to know that his enemy is not a mortal and counted amongst gods.

His legitimate desire for rescuing his love from the curse earns the support of mankind and eminent gods. The barbarous and evil god promise to destroy whole humanity in return of his revenge. In fact many men lose their life to save world from him.

With all of the astonishing secrets of different kingdoms get revealed which pose various problems being aroused and makes it more interesting further. The mystical places with its never ending charm with added new ancient culture drive off sham will's mind. Stepping with each challenge towards his goal makes him stronger and passionate for his love.

Different gods belong to different territories that raise the battlefield with their huge armies, there come the time where all of them comes together to fight against it. Now the story revolves around the myth, profligacy, lechery, magical powers, romance, fight, and talismanic ambience.

Here Ends The Synopsis of the Story...

Thanking You,

Author
Syeda Ruqia Zaidi (SRZ)

Characters Description

Shamwill – The Hero, Find it by yourself. And write it when you get it. ------------------------------

Queen Amyra – Shamwill's mother.

Aabr – A world from the superior galaxy where Gods of weather (climate) live. It has 16moons to give light. Motherland of Amunet and her parents King Adlam, queen Hassha and prince Hashlam.

King Adlam (God) – King of Aabr and God of weather (climate), father of Amunet and Hashlam.

Queen Hassha (Goddess) – Queen of Aabr and goddess of climate (weather), mother of Amunet and Hashlam.

Amunet Hamoora (Future Goddess) – The Heroine and the divine origin, Princess and crown goddess of Aabr and elder daughter of King Adlam and Queen Hassha.

Prince Hashlam (Future God) – Prince of Aabr and youngest son of king Adlam and queen Hassha and younger brother of Amunet.

Burq – New creature representing Aabr army.

Amoos – Flying blue dragons spitting acid representing Aabr (warriors of Aabr).

Ouzo (Golden Falcon) - Pet of Amunet and Shamwill

Rigel – A very bright star full of fire and lethal gases, where God of Fire lives. Motherland of Khadinamoon.

Khadinamoon – The Villain, King of Rigel Star and God of Fire.

Sherries – Beasts similar to Rhino representing evil army of Khadinamoon

King Rim – King of grand country called Cyrene

Princess Celin – Daughter of King Rim

Huba Dara – King of Sparta and father of Queen Amyra

King Canopus – King of Egypt

Gazualam Nergal– The Rich Egyptian Merchant.

Sargon – 1st son of Gazualam Nergal (Nature- Big liar)

Ahmes – 2nd son of Gazualam Nergal (Nature – Thief)

Norma 3rd son of Gazualam Nergal (Nature – Lethargic)

Tighlat – 4th son of Gazualam Nergal (Nature – Spends lavishly on acacia house, womanizer)

Djedi – 5th son of Gazualam Nergal (Nature –A habitual gambler)

Xerxes - 6th son of Gazualam Nergal (Nature – Backbiter)

Prologue

This is the anecdote where once upon a time about prominent human race back in 500 BC battling for justice and equality with god turned demon, where power was the only language understood and paying little heed to any other things in their lives. The World is struggling to unite two admirers of the distinctive universe, that's the battle between divine beings joined by mortals at one side and to the other side a God turned demon.........

God created many cosmic systems and various kinds of life. Maybe a couple of them are known and the rest remain untold to the mankind. The Untold turns out to be a conundrum mystery for the incompetent who cannot sense the divine and supernatural. Yet, only a few can explore it. The demarcation for human is still restricted but for supernatural beings, earth is a place with abundant, incalculable and infinite secrets for their visits. They rule and fulfil their desires to any extent it can be. It's the world which is superior to mankind and inferior to the creator, where hyper normal beings of the other world are seen with no shadows to resemble. Where sunsets and enigmatic end up yet positively great insidiousness exists in daylight too, which is a riddle for humankind in which not all are known to them. Mortals were honored the most that were considered sensible and forgo enough, however there are handful of people who went beyond it and ruled the world, personalities, bodies and hearts with astoundingly entire courage dole out.

Chapter one – The First day of "The Battle Field"

The Four emperors and their entourage have converged to fight for their dignity and existence of their race, who are counted among the rulers, who rule hearts, minds and souls.

The first emperor sits in the sky, his name is King Adlam (God of climate and king of Aabr) administering his mystical army (Burq, Ano & Amoos).Who is the controller of the atmosphere. He primarily fights for his daughter. He is accompanied by the vast majority of the Gods, who are additionally present prior to the fight and had set their position of authority noticeably all over the battle ground.

The King of Cyrene by name, Rim Sin was the second one to be the part of the battle who leads the ground warriors. The King holds a huge army who are expert in war skills. The king holds mystical powers (which will be revealed further). He is seated on the back of a mammoth elephant with the third emperor.

To start as a third entrant is the king of Egypt by name, Canopus, who controls ground and air warriors too. He is known for his great contact with divine connections and versatile army.

The fourth and of utmost importance is "Shamwill" who is the central character of the story, fighting for his love. Eventually to save mankind from the wrath of God turned into a demon. He is handsome, confident, determined and sensitive as well.

SHAMWILL

Paladin of the story

The four emperors & their armies fight together against the barbarous King of Star Rigel named Khadinamoon (God of Fire). Who is very powerful and holds the fire as his element. He commands some amazing powers which can bring destruction to the mankind resulting in the end of this world.

Khadinamoon is very clever, acts superior and have an overinflated sense of pride. His greed for Aabr & Amunet and egocentric behavior to stand against all gods and humans is the main reason for this war.

The height of arrogance and brutality surprises everyone including the creator. This adverse behaviour makes them stand united against him.

The First Day of Battle:

A colossal battle ground is raised which comprises of a primary segment of Volant animals (flying, floating and gliding creatures) called Burq which carry blue feathers on its body with long ears, peacock shaped massive body, dual tongue and beak which are destructive in nature.

BURQ (ARMY OF AABR)

Joining hands with their similar creatures named Ano which are soft natured, white in colour with feathers, who work as paramedics and carry injured ones in their healing quills from the battle area and dropping them to the safer places which represent Aabr (Planet of Weather God).

ANO (AABR-MEDIC BIRDS)

The second segment, whose names are Amoos represent God of Water who are blue flying mythical dragons with long moustaches who spit something which acts as lethal weapon which can bring mass destruction.

AMOOS (ARMY REPRESENTING GOD OF WATER)

The third troop consists of mortal warriors who sport dark armour and heads covered with iron shells representing earth from the Grand Country of Cyrene, Egypt and other parts of the world.

These three segments are accompanied by all Gods and Kings of earth against Khadinamoon.

This is the battle against the negative side of a God who went against all other Gods & rules of nature, whose army is not Kind but rather frightful, nasty, barbarous, uncouth creatures. These creatures can walk, fly and creep which are more like evil in nature. Coated in grey with eyes full of fire. Huge gigantic Sherri (like rhino) bodies with crocodile's skin, bat plumes and long spiked trunks emerging from head when touching ground creating friction resulting in sparks on the ground. They represent the same God who turned evil from a star Rigel as his homeland, their fiery face can make any living being scared to death.

ARMY OF KHADINAMOON (GOD OF FIRE)

FROM THE STAR RIGEL

This is not going to be easy at all. The trumpet is blown and war is declared. Both the sides surge towards each other and see such a large number of men prepared to attack with all the energy for the known cause.

Divine Gods and Kings observing such a significant number of men battle hard with all mettle. All the men, animals and creatures transformed into fiery remains, embracing martyrdom.

The war proceeds and the Paladin of the story Shamwill enters the war ravaged region, an irregular blast is heard which is made by hirelings of Gods to empower the cavalry proclaiming the arrival of the Paladin.

He gets down off his castle which is mounted on mammoth elephant's back. He places ouzo (which will be revealed further) on a window of his castle. He whispers sweetly in ouzo's ears and leaves the mansion. He hops down and unties his stunning, quickest Unicorn. He rides as quickly as he can with an aspiration to erase his foes' presence. He splits the swarm of armed forces into two to reach the other side.

During 500BC where unicorns were abundantly available and used when compared to normal horses which were rare and used by female royalties only.

The God of Fire (Khadinamoon) who watches with doped eyes in an avatar of a Critter (who is neither a human nor an animal bearing long feathers, long elephant tusks, massive half human body & legs like an eagle more like lion hairy face and horn on his nose with heavily built body).

He was bestowed a boon from the creator that his body could change into whatever creature he wants to acquire. He was the only god close to the creator with his profound commitment to have been honoured with such a power. He had lifted up himself in the sky upside down for a period of 100 years near black hole which has the main gateway to hell. The spookiest part is that a black hole consumes anything and changes into debris in a flash. He stood close to the black hole without minding his life to persuade the creator.

Shamwill keeps running towards the war ravaged area and even 'Khadinamoon' keeps running towards Shamwill, both intersect at a point where they stop and begin the fight.

After a long battle, In spite of being strong human Shamwill gets seriously wounded. According to the laws of the war, the war has to stop at night and can get carried forward for the next day. Amoos, Burq, Ano and different warriors hurry to pick Shamwill up from the battle ground to a safer place to provide him some brisk medical healing.

They put Shamwill on flying carpet as he is seriously injured. The flying carpet takes Shamwill to the castle which is on the back of a mammoth elephant where different sovereigns are present in advance. The elephant takes the emperors back to the mountains where a mansion is made for them to rest after the war.

All assemble to see Shamwill and his physical condition consisting God Adlam & Goddess Hassha, the King Canopus, the King Rim Sin, his daughter Celin & his son-in- law Olax, the Gazualam Nergal, the mother Amyra and other Gods.

Regardless of watching all this he seeks something with his eyes and after that his mother reassures him, whispers in his ears that "she is protected and sound so don't be worried about her safety as we have transported her to a place which you are aware of so that Khadinamoon does not abduct or make any attempt to harm her,

She is watching you, listening to you do not be worried" hearing to it Shamwill takes a sigh of relief and goes unconscious. As the bolts that had hit Shamwill were lethal, the priest (Medical Healer) gives him natural remedy to recuperate and give him a sound sleep.

Gods of Aabr flies around the mountains and lights it up with little lights of blue ice so Khadinamoon does not enter (as he himself and his army beings afraid of ice) during the night. During his monitoring process he asserts goddess Hassha "I just want Shamwill to get well soon as I owe him...." Goddess replies, "don't worry everything will be fine. If 'Khadinamoon' wins this, world will be destroyed including Aabr." God Adlam reverts, "No that will never happen as we all gods are fighting against him. But one thing I am worried about is his special blessings with special powers which he attained from the Creator" Goddess nods her head. He adds, "He is superior to all gods and attained highest position in the court of creator." Goddess turns towards God Adlam and utters "then?" the God Adlam replies "Don't worry even creator is watching. Let's finish our work and get inside. We need to join the council for tomorrow's preparation." Hence they leave towards the buckle of a mountain.

Here Khadinamoon is exceptionally upbeat in the wake of harming Shamwill and enjoys the devour with his mates. He pulls out flesh of dead Aabr creatures and earthlings and he screams "Victory!!" all roar with him. The cooks set up the devour and encourage his master Khadinamoon for the coming day. The blue winged dragons which are dead in the battle are roasted and eaten with additional fun and interest. They burst crackers to make their opponents envious of what harm they have done to them. Khadinamoon instructs his army that "everyone should cut these bloody humans into pieces and make sure no one is left alive on this planet." And with a smile and arrogance he adds "I am the God of Fire and I will burn this planet alive." Watching the other side he runs towards the ground and exclaims and becomes desperate.

Subsequently the night falls and after giving the medical aid to Shamwill all emperors and gods sit to rest in a buckle of a mountain, monitored by fighters with their powers. While sitting and examining about the following day arrangements for the war, the prince of Aabr who is 6 year old tickles the finger of Amyra, she bends down to ask what the little sovereign Hashlam needs .

He tells "as my parents are occupied I can't fall asleep." Amyra asks "How can I improve the situation for you dear prince?" he answers to her, "tell me a story so that I can peacefully fall asleep, like my mom does it all the time" So Amyra lifts him up and carries him to his bed. As being the sovereign of Aabr he has supernatural wings which work as per his conduct, it vanishes when he reaches to his bed. Amyra makes him comfortable and tells him "this is the story of a land where there was ...

MOTHER AMYRA

Chapter Two
Egypt and the Shamwill's Family

There was light blue sky with a full moon and stars twinkling above the desert, there numerous group of villages were present in a vast kingdom of Egypt where poor labourers who were looked down and treated low with brutality by rich in the society.

Slaves splashed in dirty mud and drenched in sweat, strolling back to homes with lost hopes on their faces and to the opposite side are the rich making most of their lives entertained by concerts, dances and infidelity was to its heights whereas streets of poor were messed up with dirt sorrow and grief.

Rich patios encompassed by steers with long eared goats, grape yards for wines which were taken care by rich guards and poor battling for a single meal, poor homes made of mud and rich have high mounted castles and chalets. Sophisticated wealthy Women went with their palanquin bearers around adorned with most expensive attires, tinted cosmetics of emerald, rubies and well painted inked bodies.

Soldiers on unicorns and camels using hunters on slaves. The scene is by all accounts terrible for slaves and equally pleasurable for rich with the sense of being empowered.

Subsequent to intersection their lay avenues of rich and poor, then appears a castle of a King which is exceptionally sumptuous and far from all worries of the general population and it takes couple of days just to reach there.

A beautiful wide peacock ratified throne studded with blue sapphire, diamonds, turquoises and rubies. A masculine excellent foot with precious stone studded footwear ventures up and sits on the position of authority.

A huge trumpet's sound is blown in his honour. He delivers to the marshal with authoritative voice that"Triumph ought to be the only word which should please my ears". As the Marshal looks up and addresses the King, "yes my Excellency "and then he sees seven pixies spinning above the head of the king and his throne. Marshall came out of the court with his orderlies finding royal residence covering some distance followed by castle leading to the landmass covered by the water body from the three sides. This is none other than the King of Egypt named "Canopus" with his magnificent kingdom.

Among all these there was one rich chalet quiet and unfaltering with no clamor yet carried weight. It was the main home of a decent diamond merchant whose name was Gazualam Nergal (who was a slim, tall old man with grey beard and long hair wearing tonic of white shading, brilliant belt holding a dragger and pocket attached to it, elegant rush slippers and tall Egyptian exquisite turban on his head, elegantly overlaid on his garments.

He has 200 camels, 50 unicorns, 100 goats and 200 turkey chickens and huge grounds of ranches where rice was grown. He was a very big diamond merchant who uses to travel at considerable measure of time to various kingdoms. He had six sons from his first spouse who dies naturally.

The First son of Gazualam Nergal is Sargon, a big liar, second one Ahmes, a chronic thief, third one is Norma a lethargic figure, fourth one Tighlat who spends lavishly on acacia house, fifth one Djedi, a big gambler by nature, sixth one Xerxes who is very good at gossip occupied all time in listening what royals talks and create fights amongst them and seventh one is Shamwill who is not like any of his half-brothers who is extremely persevering, strong and significantly gifted in khopesh , Tahtib and sword workmanship, who is tall and has got astonishing looks with beautiful eyes cinder hues with light beard and a long wavy set of hair & sporting inked tattoo on his hand, who is the son from the other spouse by name Amyra who is also sick. Everyone around knows Amyra is from another country who doesn't have any witness to their marriage.

Chapter Three

Death of the Mother “Amyra”

Gazualam Nergal enters his multistory chalet and strolls towards his room. After entering into the room he asks the house attendant "how is the health of Amyra? (Who is sick) "The house attendant answers, “As said by the priest (Medical Healer) that she has little left time with us", after hearing this news he leaves the room with grief and pain in his heart. He sits in the passageway thinking about Amyra and hears a loud snickers from the patio he races back to the backyard, he discovers his sons chuckling and telling graciously that “we truly had a fabulous time and did you take a gander at the looks of that man? How terrible he was” they begin to giggle. Despite the very bad state of health of step mother the son’s don’t really care for it. The minute they see their father they quit snickering. Gazualam lets them know that and says "do you have any mercy in your souls? I would rather be ok without having sons than having ones like you" he finds his seventh son Shamwill sitting close to pond and watching impression of sky in it. He feels he is the only one who is bothered about his real mother Amyra. All of a sudden, the servant starts screaming and calling everyone. All surges inside the home to check what happened. Subsequently as they enter into the room they discover the mother has already died and the Shamwill bewails, "mother you can't abandon us like this please come back". Father consoles Shamwill as he cries inconsolably and carries out the last rituals for entombment. Recalling his mother, from childhood to adulthood he cries with desolation and pain.

Amyra is taken to the cemetery and father reveals Shamwill that his mother put trust in him and disclosed that she wished her body to be covered in a pine box with basic traditional rites. She needed considerable a few individuals to maintain a strategic distance from boisterous ambience" paying heed to it Shamwill answers that whatever his father felt was ideal for her according to her wish and he stands by him (And he keeps on crying in grief). All the last funeral rites is taken care of by Gazualam and they all arrive home with agonizing minutes.

[As the Prince Hashlam (the prince of Aabr and son of God Adlam) looks at Amyra with a confounding face. (Prince is confounded as he probably is aware of the character mother Amyra had died then how come she was alive before him? Might be it's only a story!) Mother Amyra looks at the prince with a grin on her face and continues narrating....]

Shamwill and Gazualam console each other. Most of the royals visit the chalet to pay homage and convey condolences. Subsequently, Gazualam takes Shamwill to his room so that he could take rest. He tells Shamwill "Son be composed and try to remain sound so that I could discuss a couple of things tomorrow with you and rest of you." and then he leaves. Shamwill tries dozing off however his mother memories keep him alert. He watches the souvenirs with tears in his eyes given by his mother.

Chapter Four

Mysterious Well of Morah Valley

The following day in the morning father Gazualam calls all of his sons to his massive corridor. He requests that they search their inner self and prove their capabilities by adding value to their actions and be rightful heirs. Father knows about the Shamwill who is sharp, dedicated and talented with a clear perspective personality. He orders them to leave towards their goals as soon as possible. Shamwill states "As I have no reason currently to hold back myself in Egypt, father I want to go tomorrow. May I?" Gazualam nods his head showing consent. Subsequently, the following day housekeepers prepare provision for their odyssey.

Gazualam gives 50 dinar to each of his sons and tells them to make best use of it with their capabilities. He said he trust's all of them would demonstrate the best effort. Then, all the brothers give an astonishing look at each other having 50 dinars. Xerxes asks the father "what can we do with this limited amount of dinars insufficient to do anything worthwhile. Shamwill quotes "father it's sufficient for me." Gazualam states "I expected such an answer from you Shamwill and whoever succeeds will be regarded as a rightful heir to my fortune" by hearing this, with no choice, the others concede. The next day, all his sons bid their last farewell from father and leave on their unicorns backs.

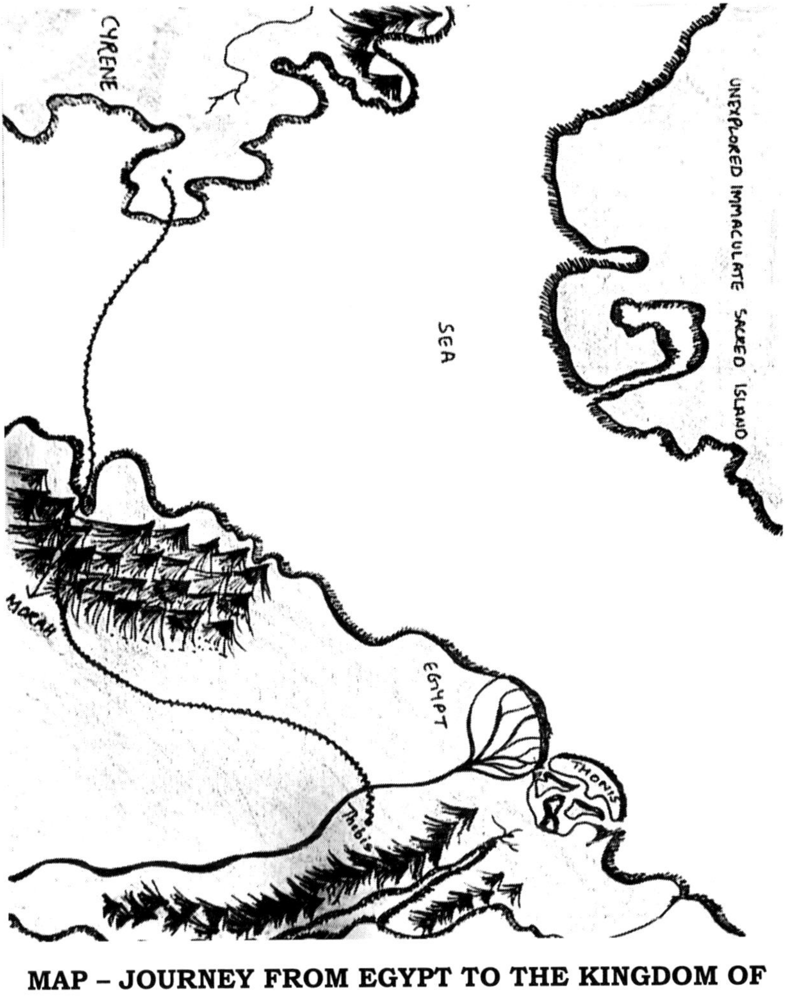

MAP – JOURNEY FROM EGYPT TO THE KINGDOM OF CYRENE

They crossed Forests, Rivers, Mountains, green landscapes, golden and white deserts and snowy regions to reach the stupendous kingdom Cyrene. "Cyrene" which is the coveted goal of all. As it's a long journey they could just cross part of it. Accordingly, dusk sets in and they stop to have some reprieve in the valley called Morah by stalling bonfire and tents.

The "Morah" is the valley loaded with brilliant blossoming flowers, with mountains covered with snow, tall trees all around with a crystal white Brooke streaming from the middle of the mountains. With moon and stars twinkling in the sky.

The minute Shamwill arrives, he feels something supernatural about the place. He smells something in the air which is unprecedented. He feels the enchantment in the air which fascinates him to blush for unknown reasons.

They locate a major old well close by. Ahmes states "we have a wonderful "sweet water" river streaming down, then why would anyone drink from any ordinary well?" Tighlat replies "more often these wells are available in the areas where there is a shortage of water. Come let's take a sip of water from the well." All walk towards it. Djedi takes out the water and everybody tastes it. Every one of them spits out because of intensity of salinity in the water. Sargon states "this is appalling, how about leaving this place." They stroll back towards their tents. However, for Shamwill it's an astonishing truth as far as he knows that close by to a River where sweet water streams down from the mountains, no well bears salty water that too with dark green hue. He leaves in bewilderment.

They all sit together and gazing in the eyes. Sargon calls his own brother's to the corner where sShamwill was occupied in setting up tents and orchestrating wood for the fire. The Sargon who is the eldest brother advises all his brothers that "As Shamwill is exceptionally intelligent so he will claim the honour of the best son and assume control over the legacy of the family. Accordingly, he needs to be executed before adopting a clear path for our goal and furthermore, we have another reason that he is our step brother." The rest of them nod their heads positively to Sargon in a matter of no time.

They make a plan for the assassination of Shamwill by way of tossing him into well while he is asleep. The night passes by and Shamwill falls asleep. All the brothers look for an opportunity to throw him into the well likewise they succeed in eliminating Shamwill throwing him into the well. As Shamwill struggles to find his breathe in the water to survive and goes unconscious. While drowning he is shocked and in utter disbelief as to how his brothers could do this to him and cries aloud for help. Along these lines he lost his wits.

He opens his eyes to end up in a lovely royal place as he considered himself as dead. Thinking as if his soul has separated from his body and reached paradise. He begins to stroll further and starts exploring the place.

He finds a large body of mind boggling mystical springing fountains, exquisite gigantic entryways consisting of huge rooms, chandelier made of smoke changing shapes and hues, tremendous lobby all made of gold and precious stones. He begins to murmur, "I feel so peacefull. I have never witnessed such an excellent place but why my soul is here? Does my mother Amyra lives here the same way? He wishes to see his mother if the god permits him to do so" and he continues with profound murmurs. In the prominent part of the place he finds unusual entryways with multiple doors where a cryption is engraved on it in ancient language which seems to be nothing but warnings.

Scroll on the door (Babylonian dialect)

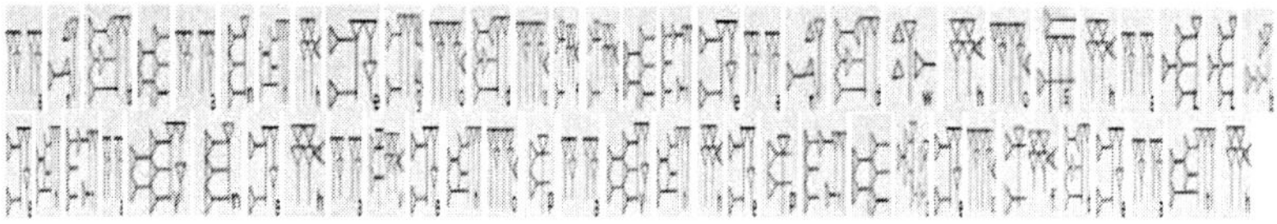

“And I am the god of fire and who shall betray me have to pay the price of death.”

Scroll on the doors (Egyptian dialect)

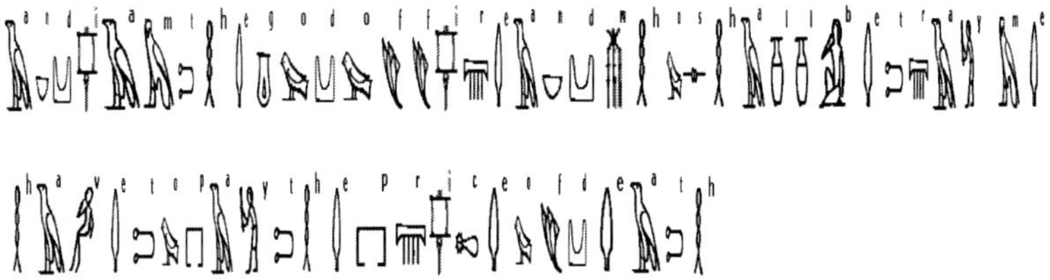

"And I am the god of fire and who shall betray me have to pay the price of death."

He again discovers two dialects with similar type of cryption having more frightening warning signal than before.

Dialects with warnings:

(If the door is opened, it would lead to the dismemberment of their heads in a flash from their body by the Khadinamoon who will hold their soul and eat their flesh to make you slave forever.)

(If the door is opened, it would lead to the dismemberment of their heads in a flash from their body by the "Khadinamoon" who will hold their soul and eat their flesh to make you slave forever.)

Taking himself as a soul and no damage to his body, he opens this entryway as well.

He finds a chilling atmosphere in the room loaded with sparkle and aroma evidently all around and an excellent craftsmanship engravement in each nook and corner. A wonderful brilliant falcon with red precious stone studded in eyes is hanging on the wall. A bed in the focal point of the room made of smoke lay there and a young lady lying on it, he goes near the bed and gets startled to witness such a young lady's body which is beheaded and rapped and secured in a brilliant fabric where he can't control the urge to get the puzzle disclosed. Her body is scattered with diamonds embedded in her jelly like skin and white snowy quills with a lock on it. Shockingly, two sticks adjacent to her body are placed parallel to each other and a transparent scroll written with fire in the air.

Scroll written with fire

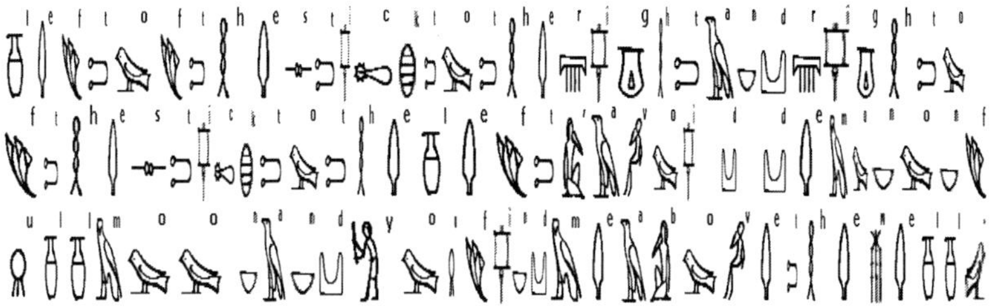

(Left of the stick to the right and right of the stick to the left avoid me on full moon and you will find me above the well soon).

Sure enough her condition remains a riddle to Shamwill.

As occupied in observing all the surrounding areas of the room he hears an uproarious strides. He surges out of the room, shuts the entryway and finds a place to conceal himself. By hiding, he watches a colossal animal in a avatar of a Critter (who is neither a human nor an animal bearing long feathers, long elephant tusks, massive half human body & legs like an eagle more like lion hairy face and horn on his nose with heavyily built body).

Who suddenly changes into a youthful human, his overall appearance changes into illustrious body in rich attire.

Shamwill goes astounded and dumbfounded. He keeps staring at the animal turned human which goes inside the entryway is eager to know the riddle. He hears a sweet and soft voice of a female as well, who is pleading for her life in great agony. He makes out that it's a similar young lady who he found in the mode of decapitation. Various questions emerge in his mind that "Was she alive when I saw her? In what manner can a human be alive in the state of being decapitated? What is happening here? Where am I? Is he a punisher of hell?" he begins to assume whether that individual turns out to be a punisher of damned in the hell as he has changed from beast to a human, at that point then will be in a big problem. Verily he hears a sound of an entryway opening. What's more, following a couple of minutes the animal come out and marches towards the exit. He again changes back from human to critter where his flesh begins going into disintegration and integrate back to the original body of a beast just in a matter of few seconds.

Shamwill just can't accept the fact that what he is going through. He was about to call the critter however a thought stays him back, he is extremely edgy to know where he is heading and who he is. Consequently, Shamwill follows him covertly. The creature touches base to a place where water is stagnant simply above him and what he see is quiet heavenly! It's unfathomable for him to see water floating like a rooftop without tumbling down with no gravitational pull with an opening towards the sky where it looks as though stars and moon are gliding in water. The creature touches the impression of the greatest star from the sky which is falling in water.

What happens next is again a new feeling of astonishment and incomprehensibility for Shamwill, the star tosses its light from the sky in the water and makes the path by isolating water and there after sets stairs made up of smoke. The creature begins to move with lots of outrage and haughtiness. After stepping up he spreads his enormous quills which radiate fire and he flies away.

Shamwill simply goes numb for some time thinking what supernatural thing he had just witnessed. He plans the same way to escape from that place. He follows a similar impression of the star and happens to step on smoke stairs. Unbeknownst to him that route lead back to the ground and he finds a similar well from where he was pushed into by his step brothers.

Consequently turning out from the well he realizes, he is much more than alive and mortal. Breaking down the catastrophe he confronted, he feels exceptionally worn out and fatigued. He sits close to the well and contemplates the mind blowing incident occurred to him and eventually analyzing the disaster he was confronted by his brothers. Because of inappropriate rest and struggle with water makes him extremely exhausted, he chooses to take a nap near to the trees and decides to remain there until the point when he finds the answer for the puzzle of the well. Thereafter he falls asleep.

The time when they pushed down Shamwill into the well all his brothers were extremely upbeat about their actions by celebrating it wholeheartedly. Sargon screams out of happiness "it's the time for Celebration, now all heritance of father belongs to us", Xerxes recommend to grill a meat of lamb and Tighlat proposes to have wine with Qgalyan (Instrument to smoke in order to get high) which they conveyed in their gear, all get engaged with wickedness. They start hurling abuses on Shamwill endlessly till late.

They spend whole night doing all bad and evil tasks before falling asleep in their tents. They neglect to see the creature entering and vice versa due to their not being awake.

The day breaks and the delightful pigeon of Morah, poops on Sargon, he gets woken up by yelling and hollering that "what the hell is it?" he touches the poop and smells it shouting back once more "what the heck?" He takes stones and begins tossing at the pigeon which is seated just above him on a branch. The pigeon flies away from the place. He sees it's early morning close to 5:00 am, he shouts on all brothers to get up and pick up the pace.

With loads of annoyance he orders Ahmes and others pack their stuff as soon as possible so that they don't get late for further journey and could miss the fantastic grand fare of the country Cyrene. The six brothers prepare their unicorns and leaves for the further journey. The Grand Country Cyrene, which has annual world's biggest fare for the merchants to do sales of their goods.

Sun has risen and it's close to 10.00am. Shamwill feels a great degree of hunger, which does not allow him to take further steps. He chooses to look for some sustenance (food). He finds trees bearing fruits, along these lines he separates them and eats. He strolls up where his brothers had set their camps that previous evening, to his annoyance he finds nobody. He sees wine mugs, smoking leaves and things all tossed here and there. He finds unicorns foot impressions which indicate that they left off this place much earlier. After taking in some fruits he goes back to a similar place to rest.

Here the day sets in and evening follows, Shamwill wakes up and feels hungry again. He wanders around and finds few fruits for his hunger stricken stomach. But still his craving does not get suppressed and he chooses to look out for a hunt. He sees a herd of deer drinking water, he hops on and breaks a stick from the tree. He sees a round rock adjacent, he hones the edge of the stick.

He shoots at it in a stealthy manner. It's one of the workmanship he is impeccable at. The deer gets killed in no time. He grabs the deer and washes its body in the gushing water of brook nearby and begins to broil. He eats half of it and sets aside rest for the night. By the time it's sunset, he begins to gather some wood from the trees for bonfire as it gets too cold as the evening passes by and to keep harmful creatures away from him. He keeps a watchful eye around if somebody leaves the well or goes inside the well.

Chapter Five

In love with Goddess Amunet

The time passes by and night takes over. Shamwill lies down under a tree and starts observing all around him in admirable manner. Its middle of the night and in couple of hours there is going to be dawn, while lost in his thoughts he hears a marvelous clunking sounds, shortly he perceives that it's a sound created due to air touching the jewelry, what he sees is a young lady coming out of the well. Precisely she is similar to whom he had seen the previous evening in the castle of the well. Since he is behind the trees somewhat far to catch her glance and he had a blurred face of that lady.

He could just manage to see hardly anything around him in that moonlight. He continues watching around with his eyes wide open, the young lady strolls from same stairs from where he had left the well. He is fascinated to see such a beauty with long hair touching her thighs, light emitting face, fish shaped body glittering with diamonds and snake sheath on her back which was only noticeable to Shamwill.

When he had seen her in the royal palace her face and head was covered, however now he can see her with much more clarity. Just Because of the glare light produced he could not have a look at her properly. Though she was unaware of getting her watched by someone, she sits on border of the well. After sitting for a while she begins strolling on grass situated around the well, gradually she sits on the grass twisting her head in her laps hence Shamwill gets moved by her act of opening plumes which are emitting light from her.

She gets up with one of her half opened plumes by all her accounts locked in one of her quill and begins singing in melodious tone. By this all the winged creatures tend to assemble beside her. Her melodious tone can make any species go numb. Shamwill sees that she couldn't fly appropriately while she is lost in her singing and moving.

A few moments later she returns and sit on the border of the well and plays some strange game known to herself only. Unexpectedly she hears the chirping of birds demonstrating sunrise to take place and then she hops into the well.

Shamwill is exceptionally disturbed as he couldn't see her appropriately and converse in regards to the related matter. He chooses to remain one more day again to investigate it. And the following day where Shamwill get himself fed on fruits, hunts some animal and make soup out of it. After satiating the hunger he gets along with his developing interest throughout the day again. And the same night he discovers young lady reappearing on the border of the well, Shamwill is again lost in her magnificent beauty, while getting amazed again.

Again night passes by and she hops in back to her world. He witnesses the same things as he did a day before he realizes that he is late again to approach her. He chooses to sit tight for one more night. He murmurs to himself that "In what manner can a man be lost in somebody's excellence? It's truly unbelievable!" As he is lost in her charm he chooses to approach her with a new trick.

Presently it's troublesome for Shamwill to leave the place without knowing the puzzle of the well and magnificence of the woman that had taken away his detects. The day after and he spends resting, plucking on fruits, hunting fishes and meandering in the timberland. With a similar schedule its dawn, he wanted to play a trick on that particular lady so he doesn't get lost in the depth of her beauty. He cuts his finger and applies lemon on it with the goal in mind that this gash on his finger doesn't let him to be careless. He is exceptionally restless to get some information about the issue.

In this manner that night he intends to succeed and stays cognizant. It's the ideal time for her to come up and Shamwill's heart begins to throb faster. He hears the clunking clamors and he sets himself up for the introduction. She comes up and Shamwill is goes to overlook his injury but it keeps him aware of the present. As her routine she does singing, dancing and moving around and all of a sudden she stops at a place and finds somebody is watching her. While promptly she observes a young man approaching her. She gets terrified and makes her strides in reverse. Shamwill goes near her and tries to make an interaction. He starts to address her,

"Goodness thy regard to the lady of magnificence may I have the delight to converse with you? Do you comprehend my dialect? You don't appear to be a human? Right?" She turns back and get terrified and tries concealing her behind the borders of the well. He tries to make her comfortable, "Don't fear my presence. I am extremely unassuming human who does no mischief with all decency."

Therein she comes ahead a little further and gazes toward Shamwill. The vibrations from Shamwill gives her positive vibes. Shamwill is lost in watching her eyes which he had never seen before with such a massive amount of golden shade in her retina with silver coating around, with added innocence and spark. His injury keeps him cautioned. She looks down with blinking eyes. Again Shamwill rehashes "goodness thy regard to the lady of excellence may I have the delight to converse with you and know you and your grievances'?" With his method of approach tears rolls down her eyes. As it has been years she did not see anybody neither a human nor her own species. Living alone for long makes her lose every hope of her safeguard and welfare. And now she just begins to talk, she tells with part of pride in her eyes and head raised above "I am Amunet Hamoora future Goddess of climate and I can talk 15000 languages. I am from the other part of the galaxy. I live on a planet called "Aabr" as my motherland". Shamwill goes dumbfounded reasoning that she knows 15000 languages which don't exists in the reality where kingdoms are less than 100. As Amunet gets lost giving reasons about her homeland and answers "It's the most beautiful and most secure place that anyone could ever have. It has 16 moons to give us light which lies in the coldest part of cosmic system" by hearing this Shamwill gets puzzled again about 16 moons. As she is about to continue, she hears the chirping of the birds and hops over into the well.

Amunet leaves Shamwill restless again, he couldn't rest throughout the night. He holds up inquisitively to see her once more. The night takes after that evening. At last the moment comes where she turns up again. Shamwill ensures that he cuts his finger so that he doesn't loses all sense of direction in her appeal. She welcomes him with a grin, sits on the border of the well and she narrates again.

"I am Amunet Hamoora the goddess of Aabr and my parents are King Adlam and Queen Hassha, we control atmosphere of the cosmic system. In this way my father is known as the God of climate and my mother as goddess of climate. I will also be the ruler too once I accomplish my position of authority after announcement. In any case, before that could happen this disaster had occurred. Long back one day we were celebrating a yearly eve of Aabr. My parents were occupied in their royal thrones with arrangements for the following year to control atmosphere, I was watching the sky from my room situated in the castle from where I saw a red stunning spherical body close to the moon, so I informed it to my parents about the sphere however when we together tried to find it again we could no more discover that sphere I had informed about.

The same night I discovered it back again. I, myself, decided to give it another try and not bother my parents as they were busy with their arrangements. While moving towards it, I found the sphere change its shapes, I couldn't comprehend anything about it. Along these lines what I see is that the sphere gradually transforming itself into a man. (It's a same man which you have seen down in the well in the royal palace. As I am the goddess my pet who is continually watching around what occurs close by my side has informed me concerning you. But at first I thought you are a vagabond and would not swing up to me.)

He came near me and started spinning around as it was the first ever time to witness a thing. I set my mind on recall mode that where actually had I seen him? Immediately after that he sprinkled the spark like glitter on me and then I lost my consciousness. When I woke up I ended up here in the royal palace of well with him. His name is Khadinamoon.

Khadinamoon is the God of fire and controls warmth of the cosmic system. He lives in the sultriest star Rigel which is 30 light years away from my homeland. He has an incredible flying skill and can reach any place in a jiffy around the galaxy, because of his wings and exceptional bestowal by the creator. The minute he saw me in the eve, he desired to marry me and achieve the position of authority of Aabr. He continued roaming here and there looking for an opportunity to abduct me.

He got me here on earth since this planet is exceptionally away from my homeland and my father hardly touches the surface. Also, my parents can't detect until Khadinamoon lets them know about it. Every full moon he visits Aabr and urges my parents to marry me off and give Aabr to him and than he comes here to ask my consent on every full moon.

Listening to Amunet Shamwill is extremely vexed and he don't know how to help her, in a while, night will end and Amunet is going to hops down in the well, Shamwill tells that "I am waiting for you for the following night". Therefore Amunet smiles and hops back in well.

Shamwill is extremely eager and short of breath with profound murmurs, he proceeds to wait. He consumes his energy strolling, sitting, plucking fruits, thinking close to the wellsprings and so forth. Moreover after such a long passage of time, the moment comes where Amunet comes out of the well. He simply becomes flushed out of satisfaction. Watching her, it snaps to his mind and he inclines toward asking her.

He asks Amunet "when you are dead how scrolls of fire remains burning, its exclusive boon which has a long life, as any enchantment cannot manage the upkeep for that without its lord's continuous observance?" Amunet answers "when I have resulted in these present circumstances well, I overlooked that I have a pet with me as a pendent, before I could send it to Aabr for help Khadinamoon got it and made him of stone, who is in the same way a victim now. Just his eyes are alert and keep the parchment alive when I am in the condition of decapitation." Continuing with it Shamwill eyes fill with affection and compassion for Amunet at any cost. Without knowing how to help her Shamwill offers her endless helping hand, he replies "Would you be able to make me your well-wisher or friend. I need you to be relieved from this furious circumstances? Amunet answers with a smile and dread that “Khadinamoon is certainly not a human and you can't confront him. He is merciless. He is a God turned monster." Shamwill takes profound murmur and falls in musings. Watching Shamwill so much concerned, Amunet heart melts. She understands a man without knowing much about her is prepared to help her, observing such a big peril putting his life on line for her. Her shade of eyes change to brighter golden hue from the original. To occupy Shamwill’s mind she requests that he play the game which she plays continually sitting on the walls of the well. They both play, chuckle and laugh every now and then, Shamwill starts to droll over her appeal. Days go by and Shamwill makes a grass hatchet close to the well behind the trees as he can't allow Amunet to be alone in her sufferings.

Chapter Six
Help from the Queen of Bats

There, Shamwill's brothers cross green landscapes and deserts. They stop at a place to rest. Sargon shows his anxiety for crossing the sea which trails couple of miles. Xerxes approaches Sargon to rest for the time and leave for following day to be revived. In the midst of rest they see a beautiful peacock roaming in the landscape. Djedi chooses to hunt it down. As he is about to make an attempt to do so he finds a little snake ready to chomp the peacock. He goes closer and kills the snake. All his intension were to hunt peacock, however he wants to eat it desperately. The purpose behind his disappointment turns out when he sees the peacock transforming into a women. All get terrified of the incident. The women asserts, "I am a queen of bats and I need to remunerate all of you for saving my life." The queen looks exceptionally malevolent with a various reptilian tails rising out of her body. With black print and blood drooping off from her eyes. The most underhandedness part turns out when all see that wherever her blood is falling on grass that part is burning into ashes.

The majority of the siblings are in awe seeing the transformation before their eyes. The queen watches them and orders to stop getting frightened. She addresses to all, "Tell me what you wish for?" Tighlat is unable to hold himself back and starts stating, "I need lovely females." Then Ahmes asks, "I need treasure." The queen continues taking a gander at everybody. Norma submits, "I need 500 hirelings to serve me and I don't have to do any work". Djedi adds, "I need to open the world's greatest hub of gambling where all Kingdoms get along with me". Xerxes bolster Djedi. At last, observing all Sargon replies, "we don't need anything. We simply need to reach the city Cyrene as early as we can, there is a raging ocean ahead of us." All mumble that why Sargon is feeling to loose the golden opportunity. Without thinking about others he steps forward and puts the demand before the queen.

Queen takes a gander at each and every one and agrees with Sargon. She opens her mouth wide and releases a bat out of her mouth which flies in the direction she intends to. She commands, "Go now this bat will take you towards your destination." She swings back to bat and vanishes. All starts packing their stuff, alter their opinions and chose to move with the bat's direction. The bat takes them to a far off place. Xerxes questions, "What's the use of this bat as it's not helping us at all." Sargon answers, "simply wait for the right moment. Try not to be over smart as it may end up being a fiasco for us". All join their hands together to follow bat's taking them to the ocean.

Queen of Bats

They at last reach close to shore. They get more stressed as they dint orchestrate a vessel or ship for their odyssey. Shockingly to all they see bat had landed and its body began evolving. As per the orders given to it its body begins turning into a monstrous ship. All hop onto it and move with a bliss on their faces. It flies and settles in the water. All get into the water and occupy their places in the ship. The body of the bat continues sailing with it quills working like pedals. The bat begins cruising. Thus Sargon taunts everyone, "Didn't I instruct you to wait for the right time." And he smiles. After settling themselves in the ship they tend to enjoy the voyage.

At last, the ship reaches The Grand Cyrene city. As they all start unwinding themselves the bat gets them down on the shore and takes off without being known to them. At the point when daylight grows brighter Xerxes is the first to get up from his sleep and gets perplexed. He wakes up everybody and all get dumbfounded about their excursion. Sargon states "we are fortunate that we came here without any problem, now how about continuing further?" They reach the gateways of the city and reveal the soldiers about their visit. The soldiers of the gates let them in.

They occupy space and begin to have a conversation among themselves. Norma states "how will we work with this 50 dinar? I am extremely stressed out." The Ahmes answers "I am frightened about Shamwill. What will we say to the father?" Sargon incorporates "Shut the hell all of you up. Let us initially have a chance to win something here then we will convince father about Shamwill." All come back to their work.

They analyse markets and watch every single stall and slow down having a glance here and there at all the merchants from different countries. They start to think about the business. At last Djedi finds a place and all set their stall for their business, yet at the same time they don't know how to begin and with what. Continuously they talk with one and another without arriving at any result. All neighbourers begin to grumble about their battles. In spite of cautioning them for repeated number of times their conduct never shown any signs of change. Their evilness is alongside them for so long consistently which isn't enjoyed by any one apart from themselves.

The Chapter Seven

Curse and Birth of Love

To the other side where Shamwill is in love with Amunet spending a quality time with her. They forget the time and keep enjoying. The full moon takes after and they both disregard Khadinamoon. That night Shamwill continues sitting and waiting for Amunet. Verily where he hears a thundering sound striking from the sky where he understands that “Khadinamoon” is originating from the sky; he keeps running towards the forest and conceals himself behind the trees. He watches “Khadinamoon” flying, descending and transforming into a man out of a monster, he goes inside the well. Shamwill waits for Khadinamoon to return. After some point of time “Khadinamoon” comes over the well and flies away. As Amunet is lifeless on that day Shamwill starts to plan her rescue.

Along these lines sun rises its head in the sky, Shamwill chooses to talk for the after effect of this circumstances. He waits for the day and night to get over by sitting tight for the dawn, he jumps into the well when that happens. He surges towards the room of Amunet. He opens the entryway and finds a same scroll composed with fire. He sees Amunet lying in the decapitated condition. Shamwill’s begins to cry. He chooses to help her out in some way. He aspires to see and comprehend the hidden meaning in it. He double checks with the goal that he doesn't commit any error. He discovers same sticks next to the beheaded body of the Amunet as mention in the scroll. He puts the left stick on to right side and right on the left side as instructed by the scroll.

The Scroll written with fire

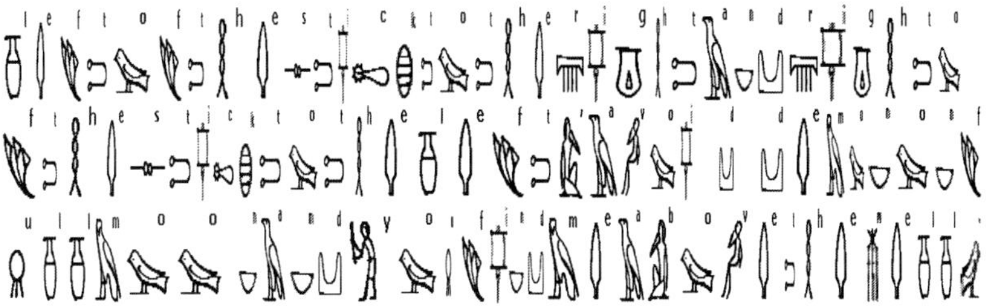

(Left of the stick to the right and right of the stick to the left avoid me on full moon and you will find me above the well soon).

Immediately, he watches the head moving and connecting to the body of Amunet. She wakes up and embraces Shamwill with delight.

Amunet lets him know with miserable state of mind, "I neglected to tell you about the full moon visit of “Khadinamoon”. I figured it out that it can't help me in any capacity, since you are a mortal. This won't change anything between you and me. Shamwill answers with certainty "Amunet, I will succeed in rescuing you. If I am not be able to do so then I am not Shamwill Nergal anymore. I have thought throughout the day and night about it. I will look for help and come back to you. I will protect you from this situation at any cost."

Amunet deduces "I know May be you will, yet can't mitigate me from this mysterious revile which keeps my head separated from my body each morning until night. You can breathe life into me simply after nightfall and it connects without anyone else's assistance before sunrise just for few moments." Shamwill answers "I realize that brutal creature influenced you to endure so much which he needs to pay back. Furthermore, about you other worldly revile I am certain that there may be some exit plan to it. Therefore, in my kingdom we have priest (spiritual entity) who could be of some help. In any case, at first I need to confront “Khadinamoon” with the assistance of an armed force and afterward look for assistance from the priest (spiritual entity)." Amunet answers "you are wrong, “Khadinamoon” is a ruthless monster, bestowed with boon and aid of ruthlessness. He didn’t leave the universe of divine beings in certainty you are only a typical human and human race can't prevail him. By any chance, if you succeed in protecting me also you can't take me surpassing the parameters of the well, which could end my life forever and my spirit will be hireling of Khadinamoon." Shamwill takes a deep breath and advises her not to get stressed and permit him to leave. I look for some assistance with nearby kingdoms so that I return to you with some help."

Regardless of the fact, they don't reveal to themselves about their affection for each other and continue to communicate through their eyes. Amunet begins sobbing for Shamwill as she used to stare at him whenever it was needed. Shamwill comforts her. Subsequently, Shamwill sits tight for the sun to rise so that he leaves to seek some help. With tears in their eyes both take a gander at each other. To prevent Shamwill from the over focusing on the situation Amunet offers Shamwill to play that “strange game” which she plays each night.

The game comprises of symmetrical cross and player's pieces move around the board in light of a toss of seven shells additionally called as dice showing number of specks to move. Both play with affection and Shamwill lets Amunet to win, Amunet appreciates winning and in this way morning sets in, listening to chirping of birds Amunet can't pack up the game and its adornments appropriately and keeps running towards the room with it.

Shamwill is going to divert and stroll off from the room when he has a glance on one of the dice which Amunet left in haste. He grabs the dice and keeps it in his pocket considering as souvenir.

Chapter Eight
Odyssey to the kingdom Cyrene

He leaves the well and prepares to leave out of “Morah”. He plucks a few fruits from the tree and takes some water with him. He leaves from the valley of Morah on his unicorn. He starts his journey to seek assistance from a nearby kingdoms. He torts day and night and cannot find anybody for his assistance. He crosses the landscapes, mountains and still sees nobody who could encourage him. He happens to see a little village close to his sight. He stops a man and tries to get some information about the adjacent kingdom. The man answers that it's the city Cyrene just that he knows. “Shamwill” asks him the route as the map for the city is taken by his half-brothers. The villager shows him the direction and that includes the information of a major ocean falling his way.

Before he could start his journey he stops at one place to take some rest. He ties the unicorn to a tree and rests under it. Despite full sun’s presence the day is exceptionally icy cold shrouded in snow, because of serious frost, he shudders in it. As he is moves towards the north the cold keeps on increasing vigorously. He intends to hunt down a polar bear to protect his body from bear’s hide. Consequently, after checking out for some time he finds a polar bear to his luck.

He takes a branch of a tree and converts it into a hunting weapon, same as what he did in the valley of “Morah”. He starts running behind the polar bear with vigour, purpose enthusiasm and finally succeeds. He utilizes the skin of polar bear as his guardian angel against cold. He lights up a little fire by cutting some branches from the same tree and continues resting under it. After a few hours he gets himself warmth as he gets flabbergasted and wakes up to see a panda close to him in disbelief. Panda wanted to take shelter that is warmth close to the fire. He embraces panda and keeps resting. Later at some point he wakes up and sits watching panda dozing next to him, he continues rubbing the head of panda with affection, he discovers something that pointed had a pricking effect on his hand, he simply takes it out reasoning that may have stuck inside the back of panda.

Abruptly the panda begins transforming into vapors and smoke. Shamwill gets frightened and moves away from the tree. Shockingly, he finds the panda transforming into an old man who resembles like a holy saint. He asks the holy saint graciously "My dear old man who are you and why have you turned into a panda? Did you want to terrify me?"

The old holy saint answers "I am a holy person and worship god in such places with the goal that god acknowledges my petitions. God has favoured me with other worldly powers consequently. I am extremely appreciative to you for the fact that you gave me relief from such despicable bane". Shamwill asks who had placed you in such state.

Also, is there any probability of a human changing into a creature? As Shamwill can't believe of what he had seen, the old holy saint answers "there are supporters of malevolence who didn't want the holy saints to venerate. To prevent them and hinder from worship they assault on holy people. They nailed them with dark enchantment bolts in their backs which influence them to transform into various creatures. They did the same thing with me when I was lost in my worship".

The holy saint recognizes the Shamwill's situation from his extraordinary powers about his past, present and future.

Without telling Shamwill anything he raises his hand towards the sky, the sky thunders and he requests Shamwill to extend his hand towards him. At the point, when Shamwill extends his hand the holy person gives him a ring and he educates him to wear it habitually and rub it on his forehead in order to get the old saint to appear in any need of help. Shamwill acknowledges the ring with due respect. He keeps the ring with him considering it as a huge help for his further mission coming ahead to locate a tremendous kingdom that can help and leaves for the journey after this.

Shamwill rides further to the ice sheets and areas of wilderness. After riding for a long time he finds an ocean to his reach which is close enough. He rides quickly to reach the ocean yet backs off thinking over how he can cross the ocean. He reclaims his ride back to timberland & slices the wood into make log pontoons for sailing into the ocean. Fortunately, he finds a tree worthy of using it and he is also aware of its significance as to how it can be used to make a pontoon. While cutting the tree he looses the entire day.

After buckling down for a long time he is left finished with a few changes. As he is exhausted and night has officially spread its legs, he chooses to rest. He ties a little swing on the enormous trees with the goal that it will keep him safe above the ground. He rests until the point when sun rises and wakes up to complete his remaining work.

With the pontoon towed to his unicorn he rides away towards the ocean. He gets on the pontoon and carries his unicorn with him in the ocean. After a long voyage, his pontoon begins shaking. Shamwill gets irate thinking that a massive fish is shaking it and he raises his sword to devour it. But, he discovers something exceptionally huge to his surprise. He goes closer to take a gander at the water. All of a sudden, dreadful tentacles show up and hold his neck and takes him back into the water. He battles courageously with the animal by cutting its limb. Since it was a blue water he couldn't make out what is the size of the animal and its source. Anyhow, he leaves the water and swims back to his pontoon. He gets to be more cautioned and alert about his further journey. He sees that the atmosphere which was extremely ordinary some time back with daylight and its warmth has really begun evolving. He rearranges up watching it. A substantial amount of rain begins to fall down which drenches him, his unicorn and the boat. He continues throwing back the water from the pontoon. He reaches to the focal point of the ocean when a whirlpool begins shaping. The roars and shrieks of the water astound him therefore he asks assistance from the creator but finds none. The boat begins spinning in the whirling winds and his mind triggers something. He suddenly comes to know back in his mind that there is something which is preventing him from sailing for which he was attacked. He asks boisterously "who are you? What do you need?" all of a sudden, the tempest begins backing off. He continues rehashing and the tornado vanishes. He sees a massive man with strong body has appeared who got a big golden beard, hair and a silvery body. He has a crown and a thunder as his wand in his grasp. Tentacles developing out from the body and water as his covering. Shamwill asks "Was that you?" the man answers "yes" in a loud and authoritative voice. Shamwill repeats again "Who are you?" the man answers "I am Astro, God of ocean and thunder".

Shamwill gets dumbfounded about such god which he never knew could ever exist. Proudly he continues replying "I'm Son of God of ocean and the Goddess of thunder".

Presently, Shamwill recognizes the message what he is trying to convey. Shamwill asks the God Astro "What do you need from me? For what reason did you prevent me from sailing?" the God Astro replies "Whoever utilizes my ocean for sailing needs to pay a cost for their lives and for their carriages." Or disaster will be imminent as they need to get covered under the ocean bed in tornado". Shamwill asks the god Astro "what do you need from me?" The God Astro answers "I need three things from you." Shamwill listens inquisitively. He proceeds, "I need a mortar made of gold, I need a pestle made of gold and I need a platter made of gold." Shamwill gets dumbfounded as he is not carrying anything apart from 50 dinars with him and with such a unique and strange request blows his mind off. The God Astro adds, "In case you are unable to fulfil my desire then be ready to die." Shamwill does not recognize what to do in this way something triggers in his mind and he begins searching his pocket.

The Following moment he takes out the ring given by the "Old holy saint". He wears the ring and rubs on his forehead as instructed. The heavenly holy person reflection shows up before him. He discloses the entire situation. The holy person vanishes after listening to it. The God Astro asks Shamwill "So what have you chosen?" Shamwill has no answer. All of a sudden a mortar, pestle and platter appear before Shamwill. He offers that to the God Astro. He takes it and chuckles elatedly and goes inside the ocean while spinning around. Everything goes quiet and still after his departure. He begins chatting with his unicorn with a grin that "Had he no platter or mortar in his castle?" and continues sailing. After a long tiring odyssey he reaches to the shore.

Shamwill's eyes get filled up with euphoria and bliss. He doesn't see the country Cyrene, but he sees ray of hope for rescuing Amunet. He feels and smells Amunet in the atmosphere of Cyrene. After reaching the shore he comes out of his pontoon and keeps running towards the huge fortress extremities which extend from east to west as far as he could see. He goes near the gate of the fortress and sees a regiment of soldiers standing and defending the country. He goes near one the soldier's and asks "Whose kingdom it is? What is this place called?" The commander (who is the leader of the troop) answers this place is known as our grand country Cyrene and the ruler, His Highness, Rim Sin. Shamwill takes a sigh of relief that he has come to an ideal place.

Subsequently, he recalls a similar tragic situation that it was a similar city where he and his brothers were sent by his father to go to the Grand fare and do the business. Shamwill replies to the officer that "I am Shamwill and I have come to see his majesty". The soldiers permit him inside with due respect. He enters the city with incredible joy.

He is amazed at looking at the structures of the landmarks and expansive markets with delightful handicrafts, pearls stalls, open wooden shoes on sale, trading of slaves, furs of different animals, precious stone markets, gem markets, cattle markets with fierceful lions and enormous size of bears, arms and ammunition and antique priceless necklaces stalls and so on. This makes him think why his father had picked this city for their business.

He was stunned to see such high sky touching structures with lot of security placed in. He continues walking along the streets witnessing all the pomp and gaiety and feeling a special moment of great time. Out of the blue Shamwill sees that his brothers are setting their stalls, he instantly covers his face and conceals himself so he would prefer not to fall into any issue as of now. He changes his direction from one place to other that let to other part of the street and while walking towards the new street he admires the chalets that were around that place which remind him about his parents. While passing through the street, one of the merchants stops Shamwill and questions him what he is up to, then Shamwill replies that he is looking for a little place to stay for some time until the fair ends. The merchant offers him a place adjacent to his shop and settles it down for 5 dinars. He provides him with the necessary utensils and a solitary bed. A moment later, he relaxes himself and takes some rest at the same time pondering Amunet.

It's evening at this point, Shamwill gets bored, feels disoriented and doesn't know what to do to charge him up, so he decides to step out of his room. The sun sets and the breeze flows by him. Viewing the City-Cyrene he is pondering over his following commitment that is how to approach the king in a best way. He continues to think about Amunet and his mother. It adds to his observation that the city is extraordinary, and the way of life as well. It is, by all accounts, more modernized than Egypt. Where females in Egypt are behind the shroud, here they appear to have more liberty. Shamwill felt very much interested in what he saw in the particular communities made him flabbergasted. The activities and look of the surroundings made him feel filled with happiness in his heart.

He comes back from his unique stroll and enters his room. He chooses to stand by the window, lost in his thoughts, somebody happens to knock at the door. This, for a moment sends a signal to his mind that his brothers might have seen him. Covering his face, he opens the door. He finds the same shop keeper who had hired him the room to live in. He offers him a hot mug of invigorating beverage called Ambeel, Shamwill acknowledges and thanks for the drink which had a unique aroma. He finds it extremely tasty and experiences a boost in his mood in every sip.

The Following day, he intends to inspect his adjacent region. He walks along the extremities of the city, witnessing dealers from all corners of the world with their stalls (Something put on Sale). He finds a hefty man over the kiosk who offers his stuff (Products) in a joyous mood. Shamwill indulges in a conversation with him. While talking and lifting the stuff up, he falls on Shamwill's legs. Shamwill screams at him, as he is a little obese person. Nevertheless, Shamwill gets up in a moment from the ground.

Giggling and laughing of what had happened, he tends to walk away. The next moment, he confronted with a huge armies riding on unicorns, towards the markets and making some announcements. He follows them and finds a big open sparse ground of the market. This way, soldiers make a declaration that by the end of the week there will be contest close to the ocean to claim the title of becoming son-in-law to the king if the said contest is won, for which an individual is bound to win the coveted condition kept by the King. Presently, Shamwill has only one goal in mind and that is to see the King Rim. He has the opportunity to see the king this way.

After listening to the declaration he gets back on the road and discovers his brothers sitting in one of the stalls. In couple of seconds, something clicks in his mind and he wants to discover as to what's going on with his brothers. He watches them for a considerable period of time by covering his face with a turban's long flowing cloth. His affection for his half-brothers does not let him overlook their greed. But, the minute memory of Amunet strikes, he leaves the place.

Each brother has just 50 dinars. They do not comprehend as to how to start with such a little sum. Each one of them engage with one another about the decision regarding the nature of business. Sargon sits and continues to stare at them for their indecisiveness as he is exceptionally shrewd. He continues to clean his dagger. Shamwill knows the fact that old habits die heart as is the case with his half-brothers. So then he decides to leave the place. Anyway sometime passes with the same routine.

Chapter Nine

Secret of Ocean

Finally, end of the week arrives and all hordes of the city, as well as traders from all around the world gather in the ground for the declaration that was made earlier. The fat looking and haggard person gets enthused to be one of the participants of the contest. Everybody gives his name to take part in the contest. The line gets lengthy in just a matter of minutes.

The trumpet is blown heard all over pumping energy in the participants to get ready for the start of the contest. Shamwill started to fathom as to what was going on and what was the need of that big announcement, all of these roar, pomp and these big arrangements that looked almost unthinkable.

All contestants are given a task to perform and the game is about to start.

The instructions are as follows;

1. Each participant is handed over a pontoon (Boat). He has to sail in the ocean alone to a point where there is a flag is stationed (supported by some makeshift platform).
2. After reaching there the contestant has to dive into the water considerably into the shallow depth of the ocean and touch the ground where there is a box lying.
3. Where he has to bring the box back to the king to claim the title of being king's son-in-law.

The king, on the other hand, appoints a few entertainers to cheer up the crowd and make a sporty atmosphere filled with excitement and uncertainty. As ordered by the King Rim the participants bow their heads to play and obey the rules of the game. But to their dismay no one succeeds. One by one begin losing their lives; the pontoon returns with their dead bodies' blood dried with unknown reasons. Their dead bodies resemble like dried piece of sticks in the sun.

Everyone begins murmur about such a disastrous game. A man behind, Shamwill, begins to start reasoning with everybody. He asserts, "What is going on? I think this challenge is especially made for people out of their minds and definitely not for stable persons. But, it is by all means, exceptionally hazardous and pathetic. Contestants ought to be cautious."

Another man opines, "Regardless to what you say, I don't comprehend that what is there in the ocean is harming the contestants and turning their bodies pale."

Adding to it, another man says, " Might be there is something about which we don't have least idea. It is a vast ocean. Our contestant ought to be careful before taking action."

The man behind Shamwill adds, "Well, it's something true and happening out there."

Shamwill's opens his eyes wide and open in amazement and curiosity. He wants to have a word of explanation to as what could be the real reason behind it. He marches towards the king's commander and wants to know from a king's guard what the game is about and what is the basis of so many losing their life? The guard explains that the game is not what as it appears simply. It has shrouded the mystery of King Rim. As the conversation was going on the king's guards rush to the pontoon to retrieve another dead body.

Shamwill gets irate and decides to put himself on line by owning up the challenge and venture out in the sea. The King Rim was about to leave the place in despair and hopelessness that no one could win this challenge, at that very moment Shamwill shouts and shows his intent to take up the challenge, this makes the king interested. The king is excited to see the bravery shown by this man who is not does not fear his death which is imminent and almost certain. He watches Shamwill with extraordinary intrigue. The King solicits Shamwill, "Don't you fear your life?"

He answers, "I dare death and being the son of Nergal, fear nothing. I am not afraid of death either even if I have to face the jaw of death today".

Shamwill's approach towards this perilous situation surprised King Rim. He starts to keep a close eye on Shamwill's daring actions towards achieving his goal gives the hope to the ruler. So, the king lets Shamwill play. Due to his own particular selfishness of getting his longing fulfilled, the king does not care about Shamwill too.

Thus, the game starts and the contestant needs to take a pontoon and travel to a given point in the ocean. He needs to swim to the beds of ocean and bring a case lying underneath the water.

Shamwill heads towards the ocean. It's the first time after having been thrown in well by his brothers he happens to listen his own name being announced. The brothers gets surprised when Shamwill has entered in the field. They started making faces with outrage and discontent along with envy. They just could not believe their eyes. However, with the notion in mind even if it is Shamwill he is going to die any how opines Sargon. So now they begin to pray for the outcome they have in their minds (that is the death of Shamwill).

Shamwill takes a first bold step and continues marching towards the ocean with all kinds of positive attitude in his mind. He recalls his father's face and his mother's philosophies. He has been given the little pontoon and the flag point where he needs to stop. He is told by the commander-in-chief to grab a pontoon and rush towards the point where a flag is stationed. With all enthusiasm keeping Amunet in mind, he moves with great zeal. Along these lines, as guided, he sails to a particular point of the ocean where flag is stationed. He stops at the point and hops in the water as instructed. He continues diving down until the point where he can see the daylight. While diving deep, the daylight begins to vanish. His worries multiply when he cannot see anything. He puts his hand on his heart and pleas to god with a hope. Immediately after that, he discovers sun rays infiltrating gently in the beds of ocean. This brilliance seems to be adequate for him to find the box.

He thanks god for his mercy. He swims further with the assistance of light. At last, he reaches the bed of ocean and starts to scan for the box. He gets the feeling that there is something behind the shrubs. He hears an odd sound of a creature from behind it. Realizing the fact, he discovers a huge animal standing still. Before Shamwill could even react, the animal attacks him on his head with his tongue, which is more than a feet long when drawn out. Falling on the rock, Shamwill attempts to make sense of what he is dealing with. He discovers something new and abnormal. Without losing faith, Shamwill after gathering his senses together attacks the animal in reply. He holds the tongue of the animal and pushes it down to the ground. At the same time, Shamwill's eyes are searching for the box.

Shamwill hits the animal over and over again. This dual in water is troublesome, anyhow he manages to have a clear vision. Finally, he holds the tongue of the animal and plucks it out. The animal goes frail and vanishes just before it dies. Shamwill is again shocked at what happened, he looks for the animal all around. Following that he hears a voice from the shrubs again, calling out his name. He swims to perceive what new puzzle the hedges are in store for him. Thinking along these lines, he surges towards the shrubs and clears the hedges from his way. He finds a woman standing there, who is extremely bewitching, has a tail, and appears to be a mermaid. As there was also crown on her head, he deduces that she might be a ruler or an entity of importance of ocean kingdom. She begins to talk to Shamwill like humans do and says, "My name is Missk, Queen of mermaid kingdom, this ocean is my abode. What is your reason for coming here?"

Shamwill answers that he is searching for a box which belongs to the ruler Rim, King of great city Cyrene. She relaxes lines of anxiety of her forehead. The Queen Missk is satisfied with Shamwill's intrepidity, so she offers Shamwill to loosen up himself in her kingdom. She guarantees to give the box subsequently after discussing it with the general populace of her territory. Shamwill informs that he can't hold his breath long. With the assistance of her celestial power, she gives Shamwill a gift of power that allows him to breathe in water as long as he wishes. She requests Shamwill to follow her. As it goes on for some time, they reach on the deep ocean beds. She brings Shamwill to the mountains where it unfolds into hollow part beneath, opening the world of mermaids. After entering the realm of mermaids, Shamwill finds it hard to believe his eyes at observing such a beautiful spectacle never seen before of mermaids. He discovers the entire city extremely beautified with pearls, shells and corals etc. The entire mermaid world watches Shamwill with inconceivable shock.

She takes him to her royal palace. He is joined by mermen (male mermaids). They take him to the room where he rests for the day. As instructed by queen Missk, Shamwill is joined by the guardians of the mermaid kingdom, who accompany him to the court. He finds the Queen, King and other courtiers sitting and conversing. Soon after watching Shamwill entering the court, they stop to murmur. The queen communicates to Shamwill, "My dear Shamwill, as discussed by the royals here, we can't give you the box." Shamwill is simply stunned and moved. At that point, she adds, "And if the box is given to you, you need to guarantee that the box should never return to us." It's again an indication of solace for Shamwill.

The very moment the declaration is made; Olax, the sovereign of mermaid kingdom, enters. He is, by all accounts, strong and good looking, yet is in chains and fettered (as if sentenced for some punishment for his actions before). Here, Shamwill guarantees that he won't return the box as he has been sent for the very reason for the box. After Shamwill's commitment for his steadfastness of his intent he is given the box.

While venturing out from the court, Shamwill asks the ruler for what good reason the sovereign is has been sentenced. The Queen answers, "He is been punished for daring to love a young lady from the world of Adam and eve. In our kingdom, a mermaids or mermen's are not permitted to have a love relationships as said earlier. As it is quite obvious in our world."

Shamwill asserts, "Oh the queen of ocean do not stop people who are in love, as love is made to unite two souls, two families and in your case two worlds. Love preaches sacrifice and it is as pious as water which we drink for the living and you breathe for the same."

The King gets furious at Shamwill and attempts to capture him. However the King is overpowered, and at the same time, in an uncertainty. Eventually, Queen Missk orders soldiers to free Shamwill. Shamwill solicits the Queen and asks the reason for her stress. She replies, "One of them needs to sacrifice either their legs or tail."

Shamwill answers, "As both have cherished the feeling of love, they both have to sacrifice equally. As love preaches sacrifice, both need to contribute."

Queen Missk asks him as to how it is possible. Shamwill suggests, "Let the prince be human for six months and the lady to be a mermaid for another six. In the long run, both will sacrifice their assigned turns equally." The Queen gets persuaded and the sovereign as well, by all accounts, upbeat about the proposal from Shamwill and expresses gratitude to him for his assistance. After this, Shamwill leaves with the box.

Here above the surface of the ocean, King Rim and others sit tight, waiting for Shamwill throughout the day. They begin to get restless. They find neither Shamwill nor his body showing up. By not finding any fruitful result King Rim decides to clear the game zone by ordering his men. He sets up his camp in anticipation of something turning up some time or the other (But in short time not days) close to the shore.

Though he knows the dead body or Shamwill has not surfaced nor the box visible anymore but he was, in the back of the mind, very curious about what could have taken place inside the ocean that hindered both the possibilities.

The Queen Missk sends Shamwill up with a few mermen warriors. They swim towards the pontoon and help him in stacking the box into the vessel. He takes the box and sails towards the shore. King Rim's commander-in-chief, who is looking at the ocean from the previous evening with his traditional long binocular sees a pontoon heading towards them near the shore.

He acknowledges and passes on the information to the King Rim. Appalled at all this, they find Shamwill alive in addition. King's men start to blow their trumpets again signally something very important has occurred which attracts everyone's attention. King Rim rushes towards the shore in great disbelief. All get shell-shocked and king is not in his normal royal attire as he is supposed to be and even without footwear. He finds Shamwill coming close to the shore and trying to take out the box from his pontoon. Everybody races out to the shore to help Shamwill.

The king begins to run towards Shamwill. He goes near him and gets amped up for the box. Shamwill realizes that the king is not at all interested in any lives lost for bringing that coveted box to him rather he was only interested in procuring the box. Shamwill shows his contempt for the king for his apathy for the human lives.

Shamwill's main goal is to look for help to save Amunet. The commander-in-chief takes the box and gets it to the shore. King Rim begins kissing the box with such an ecstasy. He turns towards Shamwill and embraces him. Shamwill moves in reverse as King orders the men to open the box. In a minute, he finds another pontoon originating from the ocean, he orders the soldiers to take their positions for any untoward incident. Shamwill watches it with great interest.

Shamwill scratches his moustache with his profound musings. As the pontoon comes nearer, he finds a person similar to the prince of mermaid, Olax. Shamwill requests that the king evacuate his armed men as he recognizes the person nearing them and informs them not to panic as he is familiar to him. King orders his the army to back off. The sovereign Olax sets his foot on shore and begins walking towards them.

Shamwill gets astonished at the way Olax, a merman walking towards him with his legs leading him to think what could have been in this miracle. Anyway, Shamwill welcomes him. He is partly in perplexity about the entire occurrence. As of recently, he was only contemplating a treasure box. Now, he needs to uncover the riddle at any cost.

After accepting his welcome, Prince Olax surges towards the box and opens it. As Shamwill doesn't know about what is lying in the box, he gets apprehensive about the box. He thinks “Why King Rim and Prince Olax of different worlds are behind this box?”

Shockingly, a female emerges from the box. All address her as princess Celin, who is a daughter of King Rim.

Shamwill is now able to make out the entire story for which she was bolted and indicted, for loving a mermen prince Olax. Furthermore, the king is astonished about the Prince Olax, who looks similar to the man with whom his girl was in love. So, Shamwill clarifies to him the whole episode that had occurred inside the ocean.

Watching his daughter Celin alive, the king eyes pop out filled with happiness and he goes ahead to embrace her. After doing this to Princess Celin, King Rim apologizes Shamwill for not fulfilling the promise he made in declaration that he had guaranteed. Shamwill accordingly reveals that he himself loves Amunet and can't wed anybody other than her and that he has come to look for help. As an alternative for not keep his words, the king offers any undeclared price that Shamwill wishes to have in exchange for the promise made.

Chapter Ten

Back to the Well

The king orders for the best of arrangements and luxuries be provided to Shamwill for his valiant actions. Entering the Royal residence of King Rim, Shamwill is honored. He welcomes Shamwill in the court of the castle with the goal that the issue can be discussed in detail. He walks inside the hallway of the king and is invited to be seated.

Shamwill makes himself comfortable and importunes the king about his issues. The king hears Shamwill and how his brothers deceived him, his meeting with the women from a different universe, how he had no control over himself in loving Amunet. King Rim falls into the musings regarding Amunet and couldn't accept what Shamwill was putting forward. In any case, considering his extremely valuable favor, he chooses to help.

He makes announcements in the kingdom and gathers all wise men in the court of the palace. He calls up by names of the eminent personalities of his kingdom and asks them to prepare for the new battle against an enemy who is unknown and from the other world.

Shamwill throws light on Khadinamoon forces and its qualities. Prince Olax and Princess Celin acknowledge the choice with due regard. King Rim gives a span of three days to the commander-in-chief to chalk out a perfect plan to be prepared for the battle with arms and legendary weapons with utmost powerful nature.

With the high ranked officers, the armed force administrator amasses all. Watching the zeal of the King's army, Shamwill feels greatly elated, expecting the future outcomes. The King Rim calls his holy priest, who serves the king during war and suggests in every function of the kingdom and its welfare. The Priest flags off green banner for his army to go ahead.

The third day starts off with a splendid sky and brightness all over favorably where Shamwill and the King Rim observe all army men getting ready for the fight. At last, the fourth day dawns upon them and all is set for the war with the much fueled, vile, devilish and malevolent god. All mount on their unicorns' backs. Shamwill joins the army.

Verily, the prince Olax and Celin arrive in the lounge of the king's court and request king to do a personal surveillance over the war as a favor and therefore the king gets ready and gallops with his unicorn and cavalry unit. The troops get additional morale by having their king alongside which makes them more inspired towards their objective. The Commander-in-chief exclaims with pride and joy in his voice, "let the enemy bite the dust and kneel down."

Cavalries move with strong desire to overcome the opponent. The day passes and troops stop in transit each night and begin with their movement once again. The troops cook on bonfire and plan every night with each conceivable skill they are instructed in the war. King Rim begins liking Shamwill as a human.

An enormous ship is made at the shore, to cruise the opposite side of the ocean. Countless cavalry is sent alongside unicorns in the different basements of the ship. They travel through a similar ocean from where from Shamwill has come. They experience the same God Astro. He shows up and demands a blue sapphire ring. King Rim satisfies his request. The God then allows them to proceed with their voyage peacefully.

With all intent to crush the enemy with their power and energy, they reach the opposite side of the ocean. Riding on a consistent basis they finally reach the valley of Morah. All the mounted force feels in the same way that Shamwill has felt on the first day of his finding. King Rim addresses Shamwill that there is something charismatic about this place. Shamwill gestures his head.

King Rim takes a deep breath and adds, "This place has sweet aroma filled in the air. Is it safe to say that it is not unusual?" Shamwill answers, "No, my king. It is the scent of a different world." At that point he grins. Watching Shamwill grinning, King Rim grins as well.

Shamwill tells King Rim that they have to sit tight for the dawn as he can meet Amunet when she comes out of the well. Everyone in the troops rest in the temporarily built tents behind the pine trees and sit tight for the night to fall. Before the dawn, Shamwill is eager to see Amunet after such a long while and daunting tasks. His heart beats fast and he can hear the ringing sound in his ears; his love gives the pulsating sensation in all over his body to meet Amunet desperately.

The night takes after when troops hunt and cook, gradually dawn takes over. Shamwill and King Rim sit tight for the Amunet to come out, however they don't see her until morning. Shamwill goes out energetically and dives into the well. Watching Shamwill doing this the commander-in-chief follows him.

Diving down the well with a similar strategy, he finds the whole royal Palace same as it might have been. Commander goes dumbfounded to see that a place like this even exists at all. Shamwill rushes to the room of Amunet, supposing that she will be lying on the bed as earlier he had seen long back. He opens the entryway and to his surprise, Amunet is absent in the room. Her nonappearance makes Shamwill cry out aloud, in affection and outrage. The commander-in-chief consoles Shamwill and requests to deal with it patiently.

Meanwhile, different fighters join Shamwill in the same manner. One of the soldiers makes Shamwill turn back to see something unusual. Shockingly, he finds a golden falcon hanging on the wall of the room (hanging like a show piece). In addition to it, its eyes move. They are as red as ruby, watching whatever that has happened. Shamwill goes closer and asks, "How is it possible? Who are you? Are you the same pet who came along with Amunet?

The golden falcon's eyes try to imply something to its left side, the minute Shamwill watches to his left he sees a curtain which is set ablaze but is still maintaining its drape intact. Shamwill surges, yet stops and watches it painstakingly the real meaning of that blaze and all is actually understood only when he sees the opposite side of the curtain on which a reflection conveys a hidden message

“Oh My beloved, I‘m again divided,

- **Splatter my blood to be cherished, kiss him not to perish,**
- **He will vary so don’t be scary,**
- **Divided by all, he will show you the soul,**
- **Pass the land of scary, tortoise is so shady.**
- **You will see my shadow profuse in** diagonal **stone of the flying stones and moderately in the crypt of grit,**
- **Find the opposite of the alley then you will reach my bury (body).”**

As he reads the lines, the message disappears.

In a moment, it is exceptionally troublesome for Shamwill to comprehend the message which Amunet left for him. Shamwill wipes his forehead and face; he believes he has a ring given by holy saint which can help in finding the secrecy of the message. He rubs the ring as instructed on his brow, recalling the holy saint’s name and the holy saint shows up before Shamwill.

Shamwill seeks some information about the message and its importance. The saint grins and answers to Shamwill, "You go and kiss the golden falcon."

As directed by the blessed messenger, Shamwill kisses the golden falcon and amazingly, the bird turns alive. It then comes and sits on his hand. The saint adds, "Golden falcon's motive is to serve you and he is skilled with some great powers of detecting and driving the exercises occurring around him and passing them on to you. Moreover, he knows many languages including yours."

At that point, Shamwill asks some more information about whatever is left of the message, and the holy saint answers, "Amunet has been taken away by 'Khadinamoon' and to search her, you need to undertake a journey to save her and this bird of prey will encourage you. Whatever is left of the verses of the message is a puzzle and you need to split it as you are the only one to solve it, and for the rest, you have to look for the help. Maybe, some kings and holy priests could help with their mysterious powers. Continuing to understand it regularly will lead you to the right path." Shamwill turns red with anger thinking about what Amunet may be experiencing at this moment. The holy person vanishes and Shamwill opts to leave the well with the falcon. Shamwill leaves the well and tells everything that has happened to the King Rim. Everyone takes a decision to ponders over the next action to be taken.

Thoroughly considering everything over and over again hurdles seem to be a common norm in his quest. To discover such place, and knowing where it is found is close to impossible, yet all continue to think over it.

Subsequently, the King and others notice the place changing its smell and having an impact on the atmosphere around making it dull. Shamwill decides that they should search for some better place to stop and think as it's not safe to be staying at this for so long. Shamwill adds "As the country Cyrene is exceptionally far and my kingdom Egypt is not that far, the armed force can reach there in a matter of days. We can rest close by," he further gives them a guarantee, "as my father Gazualam Nergal is from the royals, there will be no issue for anybody."

Therefore, the King Rim concedes and they begin their journey towards Egypt. During the journey, he gives the name Ouzo to the falcon. As the falcon Ouzo is from a different world, he is now prepared and all acquainted with various dialects and Shamwill does not need to teach him further.

Chapter Eleven

Reveal of the secret

Everyone in the troops come closer to Egypt and a few of the soldiers along with the commander-in-chief coexist with Shamwill. They move further to get consent, to look for help during meager epochs from the king of Egypt, who is none other than king Canopus.

Shamwill and the commander-in-chief go together to the royal residence of King Canopus. They are invited into the hall and the vizier attends them. They uncover all the occurrences that struck Shamwill. The vizier contemplates the entire occurrence and implores the King, who is in his resting chamber. He reveals to the king about the occurrences and the considerable King Rim's nearness in the parameters of the kingdom. He also includes that he has already come to help one of the royals of Egypt. Listening how another kingdom stood by his comrades, King Canopus takes the initiative to deal with the circumstances by himself.

The vizier's narration of things make king Canopus overpowered and has for them profound respect for the helping hand shown by Cyrene King Rim. King Canopus agrees and honors the king Rim to the visitor's royal residence just in skyline of the kingdom so that they keep in touch with each other easily.

The vizier, taking the circumstances into consideration, urgently orders the preservation cadre and imperial menials to influence momentary course of action for the King Rim. An excellent group scuttles to serve the transient nobles.

Shamwill and the commander-in-chief leave with the uplifting news to king Rim. Ruler Rim addresses Shamwill "I expected so," with a grin. Every single chaperon and soldier moving towards the castle that is given in respect.

After all plans are sketched out, the King Rim and his multitudes clock into the royal palace apportioned to subsist.

Shamwill asks permission from King Rim to leave for his home to see his father. Tired, he reaches his chalet. The minute he enters his residence, to meet his father, but he cannot get his father's glimpse.

Along these lines, his restlessness prompt him to narrate everything that had happened to him to his father. He sits tight for quite a while and his restlessness grows. He chooses to go out and see where his father is. He strolls in the market, checks father's stores and go-downs and discovers that his father not to be found. After that, he encounters his father's companion, who tells that he went outside the city and is spotted at some place close to mountains outside the kingdom.

Shamwill gets astounded and decides to check the issue, as he is probably aware that his father has no motivation to go towards the mountain. He leaves from that place and rides on his Unicorn. After reaching close to the mountains, he see his father coming behind from a great mountain. The moment he sees him, Shamwill says to him, "Dear father, what are you doing here? I was searching for you all over the city".

Finding Shamwill in an unexpected way, Gazualam gets speechless. Dread keeps running over his eyes. Shamwill falls into wondering what made his father come to mountains. His sudden difference in the articulation, freezes after watching him makes Shamwill doubt him. Shamwill notices that his father isn't so upbeat on seeing him. It was the first occasion where he has seen him after his mother's passing away.

Consequently, his father answers in stammering voice, "I came to see this place to begin some new work."

Shamwill asks, "Of what help are these mountains?"

Nergal tries to avoid with lot of fury the questions imposed to him by Shamwill. He answers rudely, “don’t interfere in my work, Shamwill."

This conduct makes Shamwill wonder that his father is concealing something from him. The father and son reach back home. Without getting any information about his journey and what had occurred in the country Cyrene, Gazualam leaves to rest in his room.

Being so worn out, Shamwill can't rest appropriately. He chooses to look into the issue by monitoring his father and his activities, as he is concealing something from him. The following day, early in the morning, Shamwill hears a trotting sound of unicorn from the backyard. Shamwill gets baffled that so early in the morning, where the sun even didn't even rise in the sky, who could have let out from the chalet? Henceforth, he chooses to go and check. He surges at the balcony of his illustrious chalet. He sees that a man, whose head and face is covered, had taken the unicorn of his father from the backyard and left towards the main entryway.

Shamwill jumps out from his balcony. He takes his unicorn and follows the rider. He finds the man concealing his face with turban, which has completely covered his face. While riding a unicorn towards the mountains, he sees that he is wearing the same "rush slippers" as his father does. Shamwill recognizes from his footwear that he is none other than his father. He backs off his unicorn so he doesn't realize that he is stalking.

He follows him in same mountains where he encountered him last day. There Gazualam ties a unicorn to the tree and goes inside the cave. It's the same huge rock from where he was coming through. The pathway leading to the cave. Shamwill follows him to the buckle. Moving towards the mountain somewhere inside, he propels himself gradually. He sees his father and a little room set up with all comforts inside the cave, along with the hirelings and assets.

Shamwill continues to watch and discover his father is talking to somebody. He can't see the face of the individual, wherein, for sure she is a female. While having a chat with the lady, Gazualam feels somebody behind him. He turns back, Shamwill stows away. He sees nobody and keeps on talking. After some time, he discovers his father is coming towards the exit. Shamwill surges toward the exit and takes cover behind the mountain with his unicorn. His father leaves the place on his unicorn. In this way, Shamwill intends to go inside and check who the mystery women is. As Shamwill gets in, he sees a same female lying on the bed. He discovers servants occupied in their work. He moves closer and removes the blanket. Shockingly, he loses his composure. What he watches that is his mother Amyra is on the bed, who wakes up as he removes the blanket.

Shamwill can't believe what he had seen. He can't control his body and tumbles down. He gets up back once more. His mother is astounded as to what to tell her son. There are endless queries in Shamwill's mind. He is full of tears with mixed feelings looking at his mother. Shamwill tells his mother with a stammering voice, "I had just you and you were alive? I managed to suffer a lot unexplainably knowing that you are no more and how could you do this to me? What made you to do this when in reality you were alive?"

Mother Amyra answers "I have no words to express you my son." She requests Shamwill to leave. Shamwill gets out of control and continues demanding his mom to give a clear explanation. Shamwill tells his mother that she is acting too egotistical. Listening to this, mother Amyra begins to cry.

After appearing from the cave Gazualam discovers unicorn and foot marks on the sand. According to his rationale, the sand eradicates the imprints each hour. He finds the two unicorn marks towards cave. As he knows, one unicorn is with him, however it's a conundrum for the following. He recalls that he felt somebody was stalking him inside the buckle as well. He adds to his memory that it was such an early morning when he began and everybody was resting at that time. He has lot of questions in his mind and doubts as to who may have been behind all this. The next moment, Gazualam Nergal enters, Shamwill gets surprised that his father and mother had been concealing things. Gazualam goes astounded that Shamwill found the entire mystery. His face changes pale. Shamwill takes a gander at Gazualam with such huge amount of questions in his mind. Gazualam chooses to keep his eyes and head down because of humiliation. Watching Shamwill irate, mother Amyra chooses to tell the truth.

She says to Shamwill looking straight into his eyes, "Those are the days when you were not born. I was leading my life of a queen and was married to king of an incredible country. We had a wonderful little girl and I have been adored for the most part by the king. I had a different extraordinary royal residence and was very close to my spouse's heart. The king accepted guidance from me for his significant chores relating to the kingdom as I was also the princess of Sparta Kingdom. I am the daughter of Huba Dara, the King of Sparta who is well known for his great knack of executing justice. "Shamwill says wow!

She continues "I was known for innovative games and tricks. King loved spending time with me and the other way around. We had great fun and spent wonderful time playing together and discussing any matter. I came to realize it was too late that by wagering and betting was the reason for the state I am in now."

Shamwill takes a gander at his mother as shockingly as he was ignorant of this side of story. He asks his mother, "Gracious my mother, for what reason did you conceal your identity from me? I was your son, not an outsider? Is my father Nergal your second spouse?" Then he turns around and says his father Gazualam, "Father and you had been doing the same thing by hiding the truth from me." Gazualam Nergal answers, "Shamwill, I would been much honored had I been your father having such an extraordinary wife. However my relationship to you is unimaginable the same goes with your mother and me that is a relationship of brother and a sister, so there is no point what anyone thinks about it."

Shamwill just loses his mind. He shouts towards them "What all you both have been concealing from me? So shocking is your behavior that changed my life forever. For god sake take your words back, don't disclose to me that you are not my father. You have been a great motivator to my life and all that I do." Shamwill starts to cry inconsolably.

The mother Amyra rushes to Shamwill where he falls crying in distress. She lifts him up and asks him not to cry as it was part of the destiny. Mother Amyra and Gazualam are in great agony watching Shamwill in this state.

Shamwill holds his remaining tears and addresses his mother "Then why did you conceal from me? Was that “king” my father? How he left us?" Mother Amyra answers, "Hang on Shamwill. It was testing time selected for me by the god whom any women would never dream of. We were living happily in our kingdom with your elder sister. I can't overlook a touch of what happened that day when I got withdrawn from the king. Despite everything I feel, smell and sense that day, which got decimation with its daylight."

Amyra begins feeling that with her eyes shut, with a deep breath and grin spouting on her cheeks. She states, "Subsequent to getting up toward the beginning of the day, I went to scrub down where the royal menials had sorted out thc lakc with flower petals, goat's drain, jasmine, and sandalwood powder was poured into the water which, I could still feel its fragrances. I was prepared after that to see your father with the best clothing as usual. We had our breakfast in the regal dinning lounge. Your father needed to play chess with me, yet I demanded to play after the dusk, and he agreed to it. This was my daily routine. "

Shamwill intrudes on his mom Amyra and tells "I am sorry to interrupt you mother, I need to ask you one thing here, where was I? Can you enlighten me with anything more regarding this? Doesn't he miss me? As I was the only son to him?"

Amyra requests Shamwill to pause. Amyra answers "Son, he would have cherished you so much if he had known about your existence for which he could have left his kingdom."

Shamwill takes it with heavy heart as no appropriate reply comes to him.

Mother Amyra proceeds "Benevolently hold Shamwill, every question will be answered. That day, I lost my significant thing and you lost your father and my girl lost her mother. It was a dull day when I and your father came together at the chess board. After playing for long time, your father got exhausted and asked for me to introduce some new amusement or something interesting.

I recommended him to play the session of lines? He said yes, then I asked him if he know marbles he said “yes”. At that point, he asked me "do you have something new worthy of claiming his regal blue precious stone from the treasure". It was my responsibility to discover something, which ought to satisfy him and demonstrate my expertise in learning surprising facts.

I asked him for some time be allowed so that I can think. He had given me 30 minutes. I got up from my seat and went to the window to think over it. Your father put me in a position wherein I thought he is trying to test my knowledge and creativity. Thinking for some time, it helped me to remember an occurrence that could get me an imperial blue from the treasure. I let him know, "My dear

King, I am ready, I have such a thing that could get me the regal blue".

The king answered "what you waiting for? Why don't you come near and proceed?"

Queen Amyra goes near the king, she claps to call her attendant. Three attendants' specialists enter the place and address her. Queen Amyra orders the attendants' by telling, "Serve king with some wine and meat". Ruler sets himself for the new opening of astonishment the queen has in store.

Shamwill watches his mother's look without a second thought.)

At that point, Queen Amyra continues, "a special event took place in my father's court in Sparta Kingdom. A diamond trader by name Arjun Pundit who used to visit my father's kingdom after travelling all the way long from Indus (Currently called India) to Sparta, from whom my father used to buy precious stones and valuable jewels. One day my father asked him don't you have something more special which can astonish me even more?

Arjun Pundit the trader says surely, "I can offer you such a thing if you guarantee my life after you refuse to believe that." Ruler Huba Dara answers, "Granted."

Arjun Pundit continues, "I have something which won't just shock you, but make you think over what god can create. In any case, I look for the refuge of my life to tell this that it is extremely expensive leisure hobby that I would not propose in light of the fact that it won't profit you in any case."

King Huba Dara gets excited and is keen to know the secret. Princess Amyra who is sitting close to the king ends up being curious and reveals to the king, "Father, I need to know what Arjun Pundit is up to."

King Dara Orders Arjun Pundit, "Quit riddling around now disclose to me why you know if you feel scared of your life."

Arjun Pundit answers "Sorry my majesty in the event that I have hurt your opinions in any capacity, you may have heard about hen and cock?

King watches the general council in the court and grins. He answers "What's new about it?"

Arjun Pundit adds, "it's not ordinary hen and cock. These are uncommon. They eat pearls, silver and gold. That is the reason I thought you may not believe and may feel offended by my story to you which is real but incredulous."

King Huba declines to acknowledge it. The princess Amyra answers, "I need to see them in our court as soon as you can." King's Regiment is sent with Arjun Pundit to get those enchanted fowls with them. With the goal that nobody poses danger in the journey to the trader if the fowls really existed and brought to his kingdom. King's men reach the destination called kothi where Arjun pundit kept those fowls in different apartments of the mansion in number of layers one after the other. Eventually the fowls were brought to the Sparta kingdom by Arjun pundit along with king's regiment. To the astonishment of the courtiers the miraculous hen and cock were present before their very eyes.

Along these lines, Arjun Pundit displays the fowl in a little cage. King Huba orders Arjun Pundit to unbolt the enclosure. King Huba requests that his workers serve them with pearls, silver and gold to check whether Arjun Pundit said the truth.

Arjun Pundit asks the king not to do as such as these fowl never eats before anybody and they have certain timings to eat. King Huba asks "What time?"

The pundit answers "At night, my lord." King Huba cautions Arjun Pundit that he is lying would have to pay a heavy price. Consequently, the fowl are served with pearls, silver and gold filled bowls in a room and are bolted under observations outside of their entryways.

After the sun rise, all gather outside the regal room to check what Arjun Pundit had claimed. To everybody's shock, the dishes are empty. Arjun Pundit grins at the episode. After confirming from the authorities, King Huba Dara shows his inclination to purchase the fowl from the Pundit. By paying a decent price to the trader Arjun Pundit, King possesses the fowl. Princess Amyra, which is me, had been taking care of the fowl ever since. I played and invested a large portion of my time with them.

At that point, queen Amyra adds to the king-spouse," I have given them names too. The hen is named Alyssa and rooster as Abell." The king giggles noisily and Queen Amyra gets shocked. She asks, "My dear king, what is causing you to chuckle to such an extent. It's extremely humiliating for me."

The king answers, “Are you kidding me? You appear to be getting carried away during you period of early youth.” Queen gets irritated and hurries back to her room. King feels awful about what had happened. Queen Amyra gets irritated and makes faces to abstain from king’s discussion. Watching queen irritated the king says, "My dear queen, you need me to believe something which can never occur in this world. It's unthinkable, yet at the same time if you insist I will try out." Queen Amyra is exceptionally furious at king's conduct, she takes as a prestige issue and answers to the king, “If I prove you, it won't bring my nobility back on which you ridiculed it."

Listening to the queen and watching her in such a dreadful mindset, king tries to show her respect and becomes serious. He answers, “In any case by chance that I am wrong, I will leave the kingdom and if by chance that you are incorrect you ought to do as such.” By finishing this, the king leaves the room. Queen Amyra goes speechless and relates how grave this matter has gone out of my hands. She knows extremely well that king can never overlook his words and what he had told is additionally 100 percent true. Queen starts having number of scenarios in her mind thinking what would happen if that really happens, things like who would take care of his kingdom if he loses which was very saddening for the queen.

He orders to bring the fowl at the earliest from queen's father's kingdom. Numerous king's men leave for Sparta to get the fowl. King's men presents the message given by the King who is son-in-law of King Huba and spouse of queen Amyra.

According to message composed by the King Rim, the King's men Huba hands over the fowl to the king; to pass on to his daughter Amyra. The king's men returns to the king and queen Amyra. The queen abuses herself for the pulverization which will come after it. The king encages the fowl as guided with dishes of pearls silver and gold and on the other side, a bowl of grains. The queen Amyra can't rest throughout the night imagining the worst to come. She decides that night the country needs the king more than queen and in the long run, chooses to go and do the last trick of her life. She leaves to the room where fowl are placed.

She enters through a window and as she was sure enough that the fowl has completed dishes of silver and gold and did not make a contact with the bowl of grains. So in this manner, she refills the bowl of gold and silver and vacates the bowl of grains. The morning takes after and the lord finds the story to be totally false and unjustifiable. He makes his presence in the queen's chamber, who is behind a curtain changing clothes and advises her "I predicted to you they won't eat however you didn't hear me out." The queen turns up with tears in her eyes. The king just becomes sad and mindful, knowing that she is also a women of her words and won't back out. Now, he starts to bid a goodbye to his wife. He asks the queen if she needs anything more to take with her. She says not much but some food, some clothes and a holy scriptures.

The king gives her all she asked for and turns out to be exceptionally irate about the incident that the queen deceived him. He sends another regiment to return the fowl back to the father in law's kingdom. He addresses his commander-in-chief, “Kindly continue with the standards of the kingdom.” The commander in chief replies, “My lord! Where should I leave her?”

The king responds “Abandon her nearby the woods and rest, she can go anywhere she wants to go.”

The commander-in-chief takes the queen outside the castle of a sudden, a herd of wild elephant's attack on the troop. Queen Amyra sits in the palanquin and bolts herself inside and falls down in the woodland as kicked by the elephants. The commander-in-chief surges back to the king to tell him that elephants had attacked them and they couldn't see the queen after that. King sends addition force to check the place again if they could find queen and save her life.

After checking the neighbouring area, the chief discovers the footwear of queen torn and trampled under elephant's leg. He reports the same to the king. King cries with his heart wrenched that he lost the queen as herd of elephants would have killed her. All the kingdom bemoans the memory of the queen. It becomes sure to the king that the queen is no more and has gone away forever.

Shortly tumbling down from the higher plane, the queen still remains inside the palanquin that was bolted from inside safe and sound. She is exceptionally restless and scared to go outside to see where she might have landed. So she could only begin feeling that the night is falling and it will come soon. Queen Amyra begins getting anxious about what to do next, feels hungry at the same time. She knows she has something to eat as refreshment in her palanquin. Gradually, it's about to be night and she could already start hearing about the wild animal sounds around her.

Verily, one of the animals kicks the palanquin and this way, palanquin tumbles down from one plane of mountain to the next in the dense valley. The queen is exceptionally drained out and nurses some injuries on her body. She has some rest in the palanquin, she hears the sound of an animal very close to her palanquin who kicks it again. Queen at this point says, "Not again". Subsequently, the palanquin rolls again down to a place where the edge of the mountain stares her. Anyway, the time passes by and the animals continue kicking the palanquin like a ball all over again.

After spending the night in horror eventually sun begins to shine high in the sky. She finds no animal sounds around, and still she chooses to wait. Soon After, queen Amyra hears a sound of unicorn trotting. Something strikes her mind that it could be a big danger or a messiah for her in this moment of calamity. The unicorn comes closer and stops. The queen becomes sure that there is somebody outside and watching the palanquin. Queen asks, "Goodness! Is there anybody out there who can extend help and let me come out of the palanquin? (As the palanquin was already jammed due continuous rolling and bouncing). Just as queen was scared inside, the man outside was also equally curious to know what it can turn out to be. Now the man helps the queen come out of her palanquin. Queen has a big sigh of relief and gratitude. The man quizzes the queen to as what actually happened with her that made her trap in palanquin in such a mysterious way and forces to disclose her identity. She replies "I am queen Amyra and I, myself am responsible for the misfortune that has befallen on me as evident."

The man asks as to how he can believe that she is really and queen when nothing indicates towards her statement. The queen answers that he can make out that the palanquin is meant to carry only the queens which in itself is a big testimony besides the gown she was wearing exclusively worn by the queens only.

The queen discovers that it's a human habitation may be a part of her kingdom which she never had prior knowledge of. Thc man makes her comfortable and offers her brotherly help. He says, "Don't take me as a stranger, I will be treating you like onc of my sisters as I have lot of respect for women in general." Listening to this shortly a moment later Queen lost her senses and falls on the ground during the conversation with that particular man. The man surges and takes the queen with caravan. That man is none other than Gazualam Nergal.

Gazualam Nergal carried me with his caravan to his home, treated me exceptionally well and provided me with all the needed amenities that I required. People of Egypt began creating an atmosphere that could bring disrepute to both of us. As all made up their minds and filled them with filth which was hard to change. After few days, it was confirmed that she was already pregnant and beyond any doubt, people would not have trusted what the actual truth was. That was the day I came to know you (Shamwill) is in my womb. Nergal with the goal in the mind that people might make our lives hapless by making stories of their own, he declared "we are already married" only to stop people having any bad presumptions about us. Along these lines, people stopped gossiping about the relationship anymore. This was a horrifying phase in my life. Gazualam Nergal who you call your father gave you everything what he provided for his sons and treated you in the best way possible.

Shamwill cries a lot on the disaster that struck his mother. Shamwill asks the queen, "Mother reveal to me my father's name and where he lives." The queen answers, "You promise me that you will never ask his identity. To the extent, I know him he will not own me and you. Hence I would prefer not to be humiliated once more. He never tried to know about my wellbeing and didn't make an attempt to search me either. If try to enquire about him, I will end up my life." Listening to this, Shamwill promises his mother that he won't ask any information related to his father who was king.

Shamwill asks "As you were pronounced dead so how could you come to life again? When myself had buried you." At that point, Gazualam turns around from the window and answers, "There was a danger of life to Amyra from my sons, i.e. six siblings of yours, as one of the companions of mine heard them in an acacia house planning her assassination. So I discussed with your mother and we made a strategy." Shamwill takes a gander at Nergal with wide eyes open. Gazualam adds, "As I made a long tunnel close to the coffin from where queen Amyra can be pulled out. We tied the coffin with a rope and pulled her out to the other side."

Shamwill exclaims in a taunting manner, "Brilliant! Then, for what reason did you both conceal this from me? Do you both have any knowledge regarding my torment?"

Queen Amyra asks Shamwill "Do not put stress on your mind, everything is going to be ok". In this way, the night follows and Shamwill is tired. Experiencing such an extraordinary phases of life, he takes a refuge in his mother's lap. Gazualam seeks permission from Amyra to leave for the city. She starts remembering about the past events of her life.

The sun sets and night falls making them have a much needed sleep in the cave. Slaves close the mouth of the cave with a heavy boulder. Shamwill wakes up and it's an altogether a different morning for him. His entire existence has changed and his identity as if something pushed to the edge of the mountain. It's an exceptionally troublesome experience for him to have. He is engrossed in thoughts but somehow satisfied with the penances made by his mother. As he can't criticize his mom, he needs to discover without intimating her about his father, as of for now he is adhered to discover Amunet and get her ridden from Khadinamoon's clutches.

Lost in his contemplations he neglects to see that his mother standing behind and noticing him. The mother Amyra addresses Shamwill, "Are you still with me even after the episode of last day? Where have you been for so long? Occupied with our past yesterday, I forgot to get any information about your journey that you undertook. Came to know only few trivial matters from Gazualam." Shamwill uncovers what all occurred while travelling towards the kingdom assigned by Gazualam. Mother is amazed and asks Shamwill, "Do you feel yourself living in the real world or fantasy land? Are you sure about it?"

Shamwill assures his mother and buys some time to prove himself. Shamwill is then served breakfast. After finishing it, he leaves towards the city on his unicorn. While riding his unicorn towards the city, he discovers a battalion of soldiers looking for him. One of the soldiers conveys “As ordered by the king Rim, there is a lack of communication on your part for two days, King Rim intends to see you quickly." He speaks to them and leaves with them. Shamwill turns his course towards the royal residence of King Rim where they are camping.

He reaches to the royal residence and presents himself before the king. King Rim asks Shamwill, "Where were you? What's more, what might be the next step to rescue Amunet? Shamwill is about to tell the secret revealed to him by his mother about his past, yet stops himself with a thought that it's not that much important for now. Furthermore, not to obstruct the two things unfavorably, he chooses to do one thing at a time. He tells king Rim that he was meeting all his kins and acquaintances residing in the city and was searching for any assistance I could gather for our mission ahead.

King Rim asks "Did you find any?"

Shamwill answers, "Yes, dear king, my father Gazualam proposed me to hold up until the point that day after tomorrow as full moon will set and the king Canopus and holy priest of the country will direct us towards the secret we are dealing with.

King feels it's a decent key to hold and give a solution for the puzzle left by Amunet as the holy priest can help at any cost in getting the bearings. King of Egypt, Canopus sends an invitation to king Rim and beseeches him that he be granted the opportunity to show some hospitality for the night at his castle, which could improve their relationship in a long run and can have a discussion about Shamwill. King Rim acknowledges the invitation and orders Shamwill in the same way to be its part. Shamwill agrees and leaves towards the city.

Chapter Twelve

The Magical Night

The City Thonis is adorned with the lamps lit everywhere in the city as it is the capital of Egypt, with the king's Canopus' existing castle, which is on an unusual peninsula and only accessed for the very eminent. It's very painstaking for one to travel on their carriers from the gates of castle to the main palace inside due to its steepy mountains and the stormy path which hides the palace in the thin layer of sand and snow so that no one could make out the real location of the castle and all that. Apart from the peninsula of his, there are other islands too which provide the security cover to the main castle which makes any hostile army to dare to penetrate. One could reach there only through the special carrier called "Jewel Pepin" (A kind of big fly like creature).It had four seats especially attached to its stomach area. Fireflies glow the trees of the castle. The royal residence is decorated with the delicate Persian carpets on the floors which looked immaculate, the curtains were especially made of silk and velvet to enhance the beauty of the Palace, the seatings were placed made of sandalwood giving off a soothing aroma all around the hall.

There was a special arrangement made for the invitees for the occasion and Jewel Pepin were put into service, which will carry royals, King's and those who were invited.

In this way, king Rim, daughter Celin, and son-in-law Olax with his mermaid follow in a glass of wheels go to the direction of King Canopus's castle.

Following to them, Shamwill and his father Nergal, and the rest are welcomed by the King Canopus. They all then enter and reach to a point from where Jewel Pepin picks four at a time and carry them and takes off towards the palace. Jewel Pepin takes all to the palace of the king. King Rim is humbled with all these preparations ordered by the King Canopus. Shamwill is glad as he will see the holy priest, who would be providing him with the solution to rescue Amunet.

After arriving close to the Palace, they enter the royal passage. The whole Palace is decorated by placing torches (light source), appearing it to look more extravagant. Shamwill gets overawed with the mysterious arrangements. The vizier asks king Rim, Shamwill and other invitees that, "My majesty and all the honorable guests, be generous to get on the flying carpets which will take you to the great hall." The king, Shamwill and all the invitees venture on the carpets. The flying carpets take off the flight and show them the entire place which was full off enchanting beauty. They all enjoy this moment in the flight. At last, they reach to the main hall where the king Canopus is seated on his majestic throne and waiting for his guests. All step off from the flying carpets.

Thc king welcomes all and greets them to get inside the hall. Shamwill is puzzled viewing the mysterious nature of the hall and its preparedness. Witnessing this spectacle he takes his seat at last. After taking their seats, king Rim and are served with exceptionally scrumptious selective beverages which are very favorable to their taste buds. In this way, king Canopus tells king Rim and Shamwill that it is made with special preservation technique with all its freshness intact and stored for such events. The claim to the drink is that, after to devouring it influences you to think what you envision. The drink will create such a magical power that whatever you desire will be before your eyes instantly. Now, all are served with roasted turkeys.

All of a sudden, due to effect of the drink the turkeys change into chicken, fish, rabbit, lamb and so forth to the eaters as they wish that to be. Everybody gets Astonished, then, the king tells this is the magic that he was talking about. Vizier asks for the consent from the king Canopus to begin the Magic show. King Canopus node his head. Vizier announces the parade of the magicians who are exclusively entrusted for entertainment of royal guests. The First magician enters in worn out apparel with his head covered. He has a huge python which is chained as his pet.

All get terrified seeing such a spectacle. The magician requests all not to get terrified as he is trained in all perspectives. The king Canopus asks the magician, "How will you entertain us today and what's so special about this reptile?"

The magician answers, "My Master, this python is definitely not a normal one. This is a wisdom python who can play all the games taught to him. Today, in your honour, I introduce you “snakes and ladders” which will be played by this enormous python and it won't end up harming any of us."

All start whispering and wonder about the act that a snake can play this game as claimed by the magician. The magician turns towards the imperial guests and says, "Not to worry my esteemed royal guests. I take all the charge of it. Simply feel yourselves entertained." The royal guests fix their eyes on the act. The magician recounts the spell, the spell sounds as if in the dialect of language of snake and sounds like one of the snakes. In a matter of seconds, all the center stage of the hall gets encircled by the ring of fire. Inside the fiery ring, mysterious “snakes and ladders” board is shaped with the spell. The magician distances a feet away from the ongoing spectacle and gives directions to python. The python begins to splits into multiple snakes. Now a literal “snake and ladder” board is created (with real snakes and ladders).

The magician ventures inside the board and requests the king to close his eyes and tell the numbers of the dice so that he can walk and play on behalf of the king on the board. The king Canopus shuts his eyes and commands the number 3; the magician ventures on 3. In this way, through various numbers, the magician goes passing each of the snake with the help of ladders. Coming upon to the number 99, the magician is gulped by a snake as the number indicates to be gulped by the snake. All shout for the magician who has been gulped. This scene fills the heart of the guests with the fear to their lives. All get startled by observing the game which change its shape and getting rolled into a big fireball. The light of the ball gets dull and converts into the python and the magician again.

All take a sigh of relief, after watching the mystical magician back. King Rim honours the magician with an ocean pearl necklace from his neck for his splendid performance. Shamwill applauses and acknowledges the magician for his magical powers and the act. King Canopus orders his Vizier to honour the magician with 100 gold coins.

The magician leaves cheerfully from the grand hall. Vizier then announces the entry of a second magician from the mountain of evils. The magician enters in dark apparel with a black crown on his head. He greets everybody present in the grand hall. While walking towards the hall from the entrance, he tosses piece of stones towards the King Canopus on the floor. The piece of stones roll and grow bigger and bigger as it advances to the king. The stones at last reach close to the king Canopus and stop. King was apprehensive about his own safety fearing the dash of the stones by taking his steps back a little. The size of the three stones grow from very negligible size to two feet tall, by the time they reach the king's throne.

The mystical magician number 2 overlaps his hands and watches the king. The king Canopus asks, "Did you come to demonstrate to me this trick which can be performed by any little mystical kid of my kingdom."

The magician answers, "No my lord, simply wait for ten seconds and you will know." Suddenly, as ten seconds pass, the stone begin splitting and breaking. It evolves into a stone man, gradually changing to typical persons. The king replies the magician, "The trick is wonderful and I am persuaded and convinced."

The magician answers, "My master it's a gift to you from the mountains of evil."

The king addresses the magician "Of what value this would be for me? I have numerous men in my army."

The magician answers, "These men can be utilized by you in the battle as they are immortal and know all craft of battling. When finished with the assignment, the stones-turned-man start coming back to its original structure i.e small stones. King Canopus gets awed and acknowledges the gift. The king Canopus consequently orders the vizier to give 500 gold coins as a present to him. The magician then takes a farewell from the on lookers and leaves

At that point, the Vizier announces, "It's the last mystical performer to engage in this category. Along these lines, I present the last mystical magician number 3 to you." There enters a drape (long cloth cover) and is placed in the center of the grand hall. All watch inquisitive to perceive what's behind the cover. In a minute all curtains burn and after they are completely scorched, they locate nobody behind the curtains. The king Canopus gets furious and asks "Who set out to squander our precious time?"

In the matter of moments, a voice echoes, "My dear lord, this is Velma at your service. My claim to fame is that I can be invisible for the required time and can travel anywhere in fraction of seconds. Therefore, I have been sent as a gift to you from the world of angels to serve you as my master."

The king Canopus orders her to appear before him. At this point, Velma look at her in intrigue. She is in a blue attire with blue hair and aqua blue transparent skin, like silicon. She approaches the king and gives him a light frigid blue lily and tells the king, “My master, add this lily in your beautification of your crown and at whatever point required, just smell it fragrance for me to appear. I can assist you with whatever I am capable of, as I can change my physical state to anything." The king conveys thanks to the world of angels. Thus, the performances of the magicians end.

The vizier announces the dances and music as another category being performed by various experts from different kingdoms. Entertainers are visually blind folded with the goal that they don't find the place. Therefore, there enter artists to perform their act of belly dance famous in Egypt. Next comes the flute aces from Persia, followed by sitar players who begun to play resonant music by Indus Kingdom , trumpets ability by the north of Indus(which is Pakistan today), flute players from Afghanistan, ballet artists from Italy and so on.

The Vizier announces the next category of martial arts. It begins with the archery experts from Celtic region, hand to hand combat from Transjordan and Palestine, Sharp Bladed weapons from Peking (China Now), Shields from Saharan which is currently in Africa, and swords experts from the kingdom of Novus Mundus which is presently called America. At this point, it was followed by Tahtib from the kingdom Cyrene and Egypt. There, Gazualam addresses to the king "Your Excellency, I want you to cherish this opportunity to Shamwill to show his expertise in Tahtib. As he has been practicing it since childhood." King Canopus nods his head as an indication of acknowledgment. Shamwill too returns the same gesture and he grabs this opportunity to showcase his skill. He is given a stick and an opponent armed in the same way to fight against.

In this way, Shamwill combats with the man with every single fundamental trick he knew. He maneuvers different styles worth seeing to the onlookers in fighting against that man with great agility like a thunder bolt showcasing his art in the Tahtib. At last, he wins the competition without any resistance from his opponent.

King Canopus and king Rim gets extremely inspired by the skill of Shamwill. King Rim offers him a mystical rope as a reward for the victory in this competition and the king Canopus grants him 500 gold coins. With the head bowed in respect to the rulers and Gazualam, Shamwill goes back to take his seat.

The King Canopus turns towards King Rim and addresses "Dear King, does your kingdom possess similar supernatural otherworldly things like this?"

King Rim takes the honour to answer the king Canopus. He says, "My dear Canopus, we certainly have numerous things in different patterns, as everybody has given something or other honour and adorned this night with their priceless performances, even I would like to take this moment as a privilege to show what I have got as adventurous stunt."

King Canopus answers, "Yes, beyond any doubt my dear companion." And he raises his brow as if to insidiously challenge him.

King Rim unfurls his sleeve of his right hand and uncovers a bracelet of turquoise with crown. He spins crown clockwise three times and after that, does the same thrice anticlockwise. Shockingly, a dewy light tumbles from the bracelet which turns into a freezing iced wall. He asks king Canopus and others to hold his hands and hands of one another. As instructed, all stand up and hold one another. King Rim holds at last and brings them all into the opposite side of the falling light of bracelet. Everyone gets shocked to see the pontoon take them to the lakeshore. All set out of the pontoon and ask king Rim, "What place is this? It's so delightful. We have never witnessed such."

King Rim answers "it's an opening to the unknown world of existence where nobody can enter apart from me." He asks everyone to accompany him towards the precious crystal palace which he made for himself. All walk along towards the crystal palace and enter the place. They are surprised with the design of the chandelier and mystical cutlery.

All get astonished with the architecture of the castle and mystical arrangements made. The Hind part to the castle is the round light emitting ball which becomes the sun and moon giving day and night respectively. They believe it to be the dream land. At last, the king orders all of them to join their hands with the intention to return back. All follows the king and in this manner, they come back in the King Canopus' grand hall.

All are amazed with the magnificence that their eyes have witnessed in the other world. Gazualam eyes just stay wide open, when Shamwill shakes his shoulder and asks him "Are you alright father?" He nods his head. Everyone chuckles at Gazualam who went puzzled for taking a ride to the sacred world.

King Canopus tells Shamwill and the rest to get ready and adds, "We will leave to see the holy priest as it's the time when full moon comes to its respected alignment which is the auspicious time for all questions to be answered."

As nobody has seen Amunet, despite everything, they still suspect about the authenticity of the story. Shamwill replies "Yes my Majesty, this was the main reason why we have come here." At that point king Canopus answers, "Yes then, we will leave as the place of the holy priests is likewise at a sacred place of other peninsula." All leave from the hall and begin to move towards the entryway of the palace. Jewel Pepin picks the guests and drops them back to the castle gates. From the castle, all gallops up their royal unicorns' carts and torts towards the holy priest.

All travel from the elongated bridge which is alongside of the sea where crocodiles gushing and resting on the shore in full moon light, Vizier tells Shamwill, "These crocodiles smell undesirable people and attack when they sense it's not us." Shamwill keeps on watching the journey. Thus, the bridge leads to a range of mountains leading to mountain caves, which are lighted with torches that can be viewed unmistakably from far. However, the ambience is so foggy and protected.

King Canopus with all royals, head towards the caves of the holy priest. Shamwill finds those are 7 caves in number located close to each other. The holy priest turns out with his attendants to attend the kings. He takes them all inside which are connected with each other. Shamwill and the rest of nobles give a long look to the caves, which are loaded with all shapes and sizes of glass bottles with fixed tops of wooden corks on it.

Shamwill asks the holy priest, "Dear Priest, what are these bottles and why they are bolted with hard fixed corks?"

The priest answers, "These are jinnies, devils, beasts who support and do evil. We have held them under our possession to shield the world from their mischief." Walking inside the cave, they go into the room of supplication with priest. The minister tells everyone to stand and wait.

The seats there are made of tree trunks and in the middle, a major round metal vessel is lying, in which red water is boiling boisterously with all flares, its vapors are extremely dramatic and take different shapes, all can hear peculiar commotion from it. There is also a wide opening right over the vessel, and could see sky unmistakably from the gap. Shamwill asks the priest "What is this vessel and why it's making clamor?"

The minister answers "Remain a little far from the vessel, as this shows everything identified with past and future." All correct their stances to stay away from any issue. The menials of the priests leave with a scented smoke being burnt on charcoal containers. Shamwill wants to know the purpose behind filling of the smoke in room, priest answers it's for purification of air and ambience. The priest waits for the moon to set impeccably in the opening of his room, right over the vessel and recounts few spells.

Shockingly, all watch the extraordinary mountains in air, whose base nobody can see clearly due to heavy fog, the passage is from the best spot, not starting from the earliest stage, so it's harder to enter. The conspicuous one is where you can see mark of a star, after entering the mountain, there is a profound pit going downwards. At that point, an opening in which a splendid light falls in the middle from the best point in the mountain, with enormous creepy octopus in the ground of the excavation.

What the priest could see is the light from where it's falling is a crystal rock in the shape of diagonal stone, in which a female soul is confined. It is none other than Amunet. The light which tumbles down on the ground isn't the ground, yet a deadly jelly ground with electric jellyfish in it with a similar octopus structure.

Initially, he sees somewhere else, where there is a white desert having sand inclining in the central point of a place with a dust storm on it and there is a route from inside of it to the ground and a man needs to hold his breath for nearly an hour to reach the place, which is impossible for a man, following it an extraordinary passage leads them to the opening of white cave where a coffin is placed, in which Amunet's body is stored.

After getting the soul, the body has to come to life within 60minutes otherwise soul would go to god and she won't be able to get back to life from death. What's more, both the spots are exceptionally inverse to each other in bearing and it takes ten days including day and night to reach from “Mount Mummit” to the next course, which is in the Indus locale.

Shamwill gets furious and his eyes are filled with tears, contemplating the potential dangers to come. Gazualam guarantees Shamwill that there is no reason to worry. The moon begins moving from the gap; the holy priest asks Shamwill "Do you have anything to ask more as I just have 2 more minutes."

Shamwill answers, "Yes my dear priest, kindly reveal to me where Khadinamoon is? Is it right to say that he is on earth?'

The sacred priest reads the spell and could see nothing. The priest answers "He isn't on earth, I can't find him as he is out of my range, and he might be in other world where I am not permitted to peep." And in the meantime, the moon begins getting off from the otherworldly area of the opening in the sky. The holy priest leaves his seat and tells everybody, "That's all I can show you for now." Everyone sit with the priest to discuss what to be done further. King Canopus solicits Shamwill to rehash the riddle left by Amunet, which she wanted us to be indicative (sign) so that we can connect it with the future bowl visual.

Shamwill repeats the riddle left by Amunet.

"Oh My beloved, I'm again divided,

- **Splatter my blood to be cherished, kiss him not to perish,**
- **He will vary so don't be scary,**
- **Divided by all, he will show you the soul,**
- **Pass the land of scary, tortoise is so shady.**
- **You will see my shadow profuse in diagonal stone of the flying stones and moderately in the crypt of grit,**
- **Find the opposite of the alley then you will reach my bury (body)."**

The priest answers that the mountain which he had seen are dark coloured vapours, which is, no doubt mountains made of coal or something similar to it. Notwithstanding what is mentioned in the parchment, it expresses the same. The cubic is only the crystal or diamond.

The place which is scary remains unsolved. Disregarding, pausing and hanging at one point he chooses to continue. The King Rim tries getting some information about the place. The priest closes his eyes and enchants few verses and states, "One is towards the Northeast, where the bird Ouzo will lead all of you and another is towards the Southwest only inverse of the heading as expressed in the parchment. I am sure Ouzo will find the rest as he is a part of this mission."

After listening to the complete discussion and suggestions, king Canopus adds, "How about we go back and rest for the night. We will assemble tomorrow at my royal residence to talk about the further plan and discuss in detail." Everybody takes blessing from the holy priest and leave from the caves. The carts takes them back to the castles and the royal residences. In spite of the fact that they came back, they end up anxious reasoning about the issue.

It's particularly Shamwill, who can't rest throughout the night thinking over Amunet. He spends all evenings conversing with the falcon Ouzo. At last, the sun rises and Shamwill falls asleep. One of the attendants knocks the door of Shamwill. He gets up and opens the door. The servant answers, "Capo, the soldier from the royal residence of king Rim, has come to see you." Shamwill answers, "Welcome him and with all respect, let him join our guest room. Inform him that I will join him soon. What's more, ensure you serve him with the best food and beverages." The attendant gestures her head and leaves the room.

Shamwill prepares for the meeting and descends from his room to join the soldier. In the interim, the attendant's serve the soldier with best food and beverages. Shamwill joins him on the table, have his lunch with him and they both have a chat about devour at Thonis with sips of tea. In this way, both leave for meeting organized at the castle.

King Rim and King Canopus sit waiting for the gathering of all the royals at a special lounge for the discussion, which is headed by the king Canopus. At last, all accumulate and the meeting begins. All present their yields verily recorded to contribute for the adventure and war. An exceptional power is designated to deal with the mission and uncommon maps are orchestrated.

King Canopus offers his royal flying carpets, Jewel Pepin's, soldiers, arms, talismans and supernatural forces. He then apologizes to everyone as he can't be a part of journey. However, he assured that he will join them if necessary. Shamwill requests king Canopus, at last he adds, and "I will join you once you find Amunet".

Shamwill answers, "Yet, how can I pass it on to you?"

King Canopus states, "You don't have to, as I will come to know through the "future bowl" of the priest". Shamwill grins and keeps on discussing with the vizier about the maps. King Rim offers his army, enchanted adornments and mammoth war animals (especially trained for war) from his kingdom. Shamwill states, the kings that he has a book for his mission, in which such mountains exists in the Northeast rural areas and with the assistance of Ouzo, he can find it. He displays the book before all, which demonstrates the guide and course to reach, and when they can. Shamwill begins dealing with the maps and courses that can take him to his adoration.

King Rim asks Shamwill, “From where he got the book?” He answers that it was from his father's book rack.

King Rim asks, "How come?"

Shamwill answers, "As he ventures a lot, perhaps he may make use of his trips."

King Canopus adds, “It will be extremely useful, as it shows every neighbouring village during the mission." All nods their heads for the sources of information that they have now.

Chapter Thirteen

The Journey from the Egypt towards Mount Mummit

Map – Journey from Egypt to Mount Mummit

The day has come where Shamwill needs to begin his mission to rescue Amunet. Standing in thc balcony of his chalet, he is deeply engrossed in his thoughts where his hair fly with the streaming breeze and keeps touching his nose and ears. With the desires emerging and expectations of endless love for Amunet flows from his grey eyes, he grins and takes deep sigh and expresses sadness through his eyes. He recalls the innocent eyes of Amunet and her delicate smile. Gazualam comes from behind, and places his hand on his shoulder, he expresses solace and presents few words of comfort by telling, "Don't be sad Shamwill, there is no reason to worry. We all, are with you." Shamwill replies "I trust you, father."

The very next moment, he hears the trotting of unicorns. Looking past the door of chalet, he sees troops walking from the streets outside the chalet. He intends to tell Gazualam Nergal, "Father, I figure I ought to prepare currently, even vizier would come in some time." Gazualam nods his head and remains in the balcony pondering over the journey. Shamwill walks towards his room to take up further course of action. Gazualam orders the attendants to help Shamwill in his packing and arrangements.

In a while, vizier reaches the chalet. Gazualam addresses vizier from the balcony "Vizier, He is preparing for the mission." Vizier bows his head and grins out of respect. Gazualam adds "Vizier kindly come in and have a seat until he joins you." An attendant opens the entryway and invites Vizier inside. Vizier is presented with soup, tea and dates. Gazualam comes down to have a discussion and greets Vizier.

After having few words with Gazualam, Vizier says "Gazualam Nergal, why don't you accompany us? Your experience in travelling worldwide would help us in getting the right direction and it would be a great moral support for Shamwill as well."

Verily, Shamwill enters the guest hall. He hears vizier requesting Gazualam to come with them. Shamwill greets Vizier and adds, "Father, I agree with Vizier, from the bottom of my heart, I need you to be with me in this difficult and unusual mission. Please, I insist."

Gazualam agrees at last. He requests that all hold back so he prepares for the packing. Both wait for Gazualam to prepare. Soon, Gazualam gets along with them on their chariots and unicorns to join the troop. He turns towards Shamwill on the chariot and tells, "Shamwill we have to see your mother and take her blessings for the mission for final goodbye before leaving the city". Shamwill begs pardon and realizes the reality.

They tell Vizier that they will join them outside the outskirts of the city in a couple of minutes. Vizier agrees and proceeds with the troop. Gazualam and Shamwill torts towards the caves and to see mother Amyra. Amyra continues to supplicate in her prayer room. The attendants request Shamwill and Gazualam to wait as she is about to complete her prayers. Mother Amyra seeks the reason for visit, as during day time, it's risky to visit the mountains and could raise the chances of revelation of her existence to the entire world and especially her enemies.

Shamwill and Gazualam assure Amyra that nobody had seen them. Both take last farewells and leave from the mountains.

They join the troops outside the city, where they march the armed forces towards the city of Sinai, covering some distance towards their destination, Where Ouzo is leading alongside. All army march towards Sinai as directed by Ouzo, as disclosed by the holy priest and signaled by the goddess Amunet. The army walk each day for 16 hours and rest 8 hours around evening time.

Steady travelling of 250 kilometers is exceptionally tiring for the army, yet they keep their hopes alive. Desire of watching the goddess and women from the other world keeps their hopes fruit bearing, eventually marching with the biggest reason that wicked “Khadinamoon” which can be a catastrophe to the world and humanity, instills fear in the hearts of army which could bring one day a destruction to the whole mankind. Each day passes and Shamwill’s continues to be anxious about Amunet and for her current condition.

King Rim continues viewing Shamwill before the mission and on one night, when Shamwill is resting outside the tent watching open sky, the king Rim approaches and asks Shamwill, "How are you, young fellow?" Shamwill rearranges his condition the minute he sees the King Rim. He offers him a place to sit.

The King Rim and Shamwill sits together side by side. The King offers him a mug of soup. Shamwill acknowledges it and they begin to talk.

Shamwill tells the king, "Isn't this journey too long? We should be well prepared and continue gathering sustenance, as, at few places we may not have it." King Rim answers, "Better believe it's actually needed to add to my words, not to worry as everything will end up great. We will fight until triumph." Saying so, king Rim walks off.

Chapter Fourteen

Caves of Misr Al Safer (Amman)

The following day takes after, and all set towards Amman, which is a part of Egypt during the rule of King Canopus and secured by trail of mountains called Misr Al Safer. Misr Al Safer comprise of caves made by the tribal groups.

The reason for making these caves is to maintain a strategic distance from outsiders in the clan and the activities can be constrained for the travelers to remain inside the range and continue with their journey. According to their beliefs outsiders are not permitted in their culture, customs and traditions which they want to be a secretive treasure of civilizations for rest of the world. After travelling for so long and heading towards the vast range of mountains, the army starts setting up camps for the night in one of the mountain caves. The caves look great with warm ambience, making them an ideal place to rest for the night. The camps are set up and food is served for all. Shamwill gets exhausted, sitting and travelling continuously, he chooses to practice his martial arts every day to remain physically fit. Observing every ancient places during his journey, he admires the beauty of the world. Gazualam knows a lot about the places as he travelled many times through there. Ouzo sets off in the sky to see if there is any danger around and in the hollow and rugged terrains of mountains to provide surveillance to the army, nobles and the kings are not endangered in any way and safety of the cavalry is not compromised at any cost.

Chapter Fifteen

Shun-Urr, Gateway to the world of sands (Mesopotamia/Iraq)

In this way, day breaks and all set for their journey. After long journey they reach Mesopotamia, which is now called as Iraq, the world's first reported place of colonization and technologically very advanced in its time. People were occupied in working and shepherds are occupied with their herds grazing. The army reach at a place called "Shunn Urr", which is an old landmark of Mesopotamia. The place looks very secretive and mysterious to everyone.

The sand blows making shapes and dash against the mounted force as though demonstrating something or attempting to hurt. Shamwill gets startled at it. Gazualam addresses all, "I have been to this place for a few times. Nobody needs to feel stressed, it's the gateway to the world of God of sands. He turns towards King Rim, Shamwill and reveals to them that, "We simply need to give them a sign that we have not come here to enter their world and we are simply travelers, so that they cause no damage."

Shamwill questions "How is that possible? We don't know how to signal them. As far as I could see this place has only few resources (camels and water) from which we can eat and drink."

Gazualam tells, "Not to worry, as you climb the stairs on the specific best of place you locate a profound well which is precisely the passage of the world underneath its depth.

It's engraved on the stone. “If by chance, you are a traveler, you have to pull water, drink it and abandon, trespassing on anything from the above or in case that you want to enter their world you have to drop a hammer, which is placed precisely alongside the well, it will be considered as a violation of law, mischief or waging of war from the trespasser." Gazualam adds, “We simply need to go there and pull some water to drink. They will grant us the permission to spend night peacefully after getting the message. “Shunn Urr” monument is a well, which is a home to 500 stairs to climb and an additional 5000 mystical stairs which lead inside the well, every stair has its furious nature to the individual who endeavors to get to the base of the well. It was designed and planned by the gods of sands for the prohibition of trespassers."

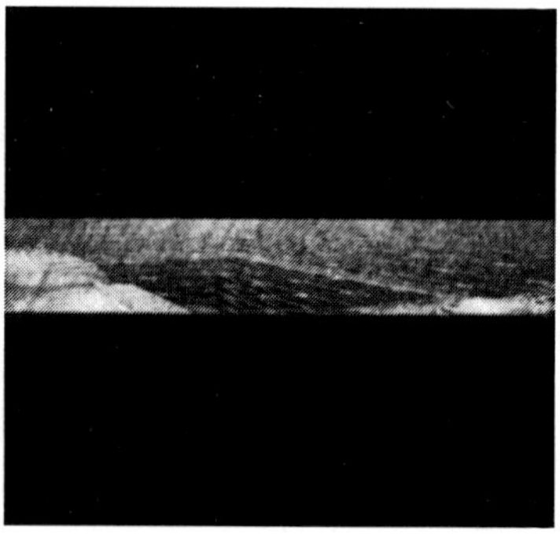

Shun Urr-Mesopotamia (The gateway to the world of Gods of sand)

Shamwill steps up in order to pull the water. He gets down from the unicorn and puts his step on the stairs of “Shunn Urr”. Without getting down the well as little possible, he throws a water sack into the well. He takes out the water and Shamwill makes a clear declaration that, "I am Shamwill Nergal. I, my companions and the mounted army are travelers, we simply need to spent a single night for some rest. I hope you received our message. According to the custom of the well, I have filled the water as it's needed to quench the thirst of my people. Much obliged to you." By taking the water he gets down from the well. The minute he starts to step down, the sands quit blowing. Gazualam answers "I think the message has been conveyed."

Everyone takes a sigh of solace and sets their camps to rest. A couple of soldiers keep running to hunt the camels located near the well to set their dinner for the night, they accumulate food for the following day as well. The camps are set and lighted. Shamwill and vizier discuss the maps to go further. In the meantime, King Rim and Gazualam Nergal rest for some time in their tents. After waking up from a sound sleep, they get fresh for the evening.

He requests his commander to organize a program for their entertainment to escape tiresomeness of long journey. Vizier brings up to the notice of King Rim that there is a tribe of Tasawwuf (Sufi) close by, and they are holy people who are skilled performers and intellectuals. King Rim orders vizier to leave instantly with few soldiers to arrange them for the night. Shamwill continues to stare at the king. King Rim asks Shamwill, "What are you staring at?"

Shamwill answers, "I generally observe kings having a fabulous time, associated with an extensive amount of prudence and wickedness. But, you are so simple, sensitive and god-oriented human."

King Rim answers "If I give something from that will set good example of my personality and that will be remembered as one of my honest deeds. If at all, I do awful deeds, for example, obscene acts that will tarnish my image as a King. Yes, off Course and it will be followed in my underhanded deeds. If some day, god forbid! Any disaster strikes my kingdom due to my acts, then I want to be with less burden of sins before the creator when I am no more." This philosophy of this kind moved Shamwill and commended the king and king reciprocates the same.

Everyone gets occupied in carrying out different activities until the dinner arrangements are made. The vizier returns to the king with a gathering of Sufi entertainers. King Rim orders the vizier to organize delicacies and tents for the Sufi saints. Five tables are arranged, consisting different of types of delicacies which are presented on the tables, in which, one is exclusively organized for the imperial camp of king and his royals, and the other one for the army and the rest for the Tasawwuf saints.

Camels are broiled and delicious kebabs are made out of them, with lots of cream spread and vegetables stew, servings of mixed greens, steaks and hot breads set up by the royal cooks. Besides, their customary drink of Ambeel is served for relieving and soothing effect of meat, which is also a traditional drink of “Cyrene city”.

The occasion of entertainment starts when Tasawwuf begin playing out their raised head movements, music and dance. Watching the performances, all get doped with such an established and peculiar melodious music. At that point, King Rim tells everyone that, "We are happy to have such a polished entertainers with such an extraordinary talent that have engaged us and illuminated our spirits tonight.”

The leader of the Mutasawwuf then answers, "we are elated that we got a privilege to entertain you with our performance."

King Rim nods his head consequently of his acknowledgment and addresses vizier, “Take them with the due respect." The Sufi entertainers thank the king and leave with the vizier to be bestowed with several gifts.

Now, it's middle of the night when Shamwill is lying on a rock present close to his tent and continues to watch the sky. He sees a fast quick light passing towards the well. He begins following that, Watching Shamwill running, King Rim requests that his soldiers to look into the matter.

Shamwill anxiously climbs the stairs of “Shunn Urr” and reaches the well. He sees that the entire well is illuminated with glitter in the water from within. Shamwill yells "Who is there?” A ray of light comes out of those glitter, after which he sees three men emanating the orange light with sparks, who have emerged from the well. Shamwill asks "Who are you? I followed the light and reached here." One of them answers, “We are Gods of Sand, this one is my child, and other is the Guard of the gate. We heard the Mutasawwuf music and came to see the occasion. Your army and nobles appears to be from a decent kingdom!” Shamwill answers, “Yes, we are indeed. We are travelers passing by for some work. It's really an honour to see you.” Sooner, the army joins Shamwill. Shamwill assures vizier that there is nothing to worry about. Subsequently, after hearing this army keeps back their swords in their sheaths.

The God of sand and his companions return to the well with the smile on their faces. Shamwill and the army descend from “Shunn Urr” towards the camps. King Rim questions Shamwill, "What happened there? Is everything okay?" Shamwill answers "Yes, my lord those were the divine forces and the gods of sand. I followed them to see from where the light originated." King Rim addresses all, "We have a couple of hours left to leave. Consequently, everyone takes a few hours of rest as toward the beginning of the day, we will begin the journey. So disperse." Everyone winds up and returns to their tents.

Morning gazes and all begin to pack up from the place. One by one all camels, chariots, unicorns and stuffs are taken forth. The journey begins again for Shamwill. They pass through deserts, mountains and landscapes with the same routine as usual.

Chapter Sixteen

The Wrath on Shahr e Aab (Persia/Iran)

Following seven days of journey, they march to one of the beautiful cities of Persia known by the name "Shahr-e-Aab" (city of water), which appeared to be culturally advanced in all aspects as compared to the rest of the kingdoms explored by Shamwill. The city was rich with flawless stock of carpets, articles and so on. King Rim, Gazualam and other royals whisper to their men to buy a few articles and carpets for their royal residences and chalets soon after they set up their camps for the night. The king chooses to set up the camps in the outskirts of the city.

The Persian priest of the city gets information about the King and royals that have halted close by during their journey. With a couple of valuable gifts, he visits the camps of King Rim. The vizier informs the king and other royals about the visit of Persian priest. All come together at a camp of King. King solicits the reason for visit of the Persian priest. The Persian priest answers "His Highness, we are honoured with your valuable presence. May I help you with anything?"

King Rim answers, "I know you may be worried about our visit. Please don't be. We are on a journey and simply halted to rest with our army for the desired time."

The Persian priest takes a sigh of relief as he was imagining that the king came to defeat their kingdom. The Priest offers the king, couple of valuable gifts from his side. The

King acknowledges the gifts and informs him that his army will rest for a night and leave the very next morning.

The Persian priest leaves with the information. Then he visits the castle of Persian king and informs him about the visit of Majestic king Rim. The Persian king prepares for the honour in his highness. He visit's the camps of the King and his men. The vizier informs King Rim about the visit of the Persian king. All gather at the visitor's camp to meet the Persian king. The kings welcome each other.

All guests and visitors are presented with refreshments. The Persian king tells King Rim "My dear friend, I generally needed to meet you as I heard such numerous stories of your triumphs and so, I wanted to see such brave warrior who vanquished such a large number of kingdoms."

King Rim answers, "Thank you, dear friend. I just took after my gut feeling".

The Persian king asks him, "I request you all to have your presence in my royal residence during your stay than staying anywhere else".

King Rim answers, "I am honoured, yet it's only a matter of one night and we will definitely find it more comfortable being here."

The Persian king answers, "I would be obliged if you accept to be our guest, I provide you with all comforts present in my kingdom, but for the same I don't force you since you are a great king. I want you to include my armed forces to with your for your extra safety, my dear king."

King Rim answers, “It's not required. We have enough army thousands in number to secure ourselves".

The Persian king replies, “It's not about that, my dear king. We have an issue outside the Shahr-e-Aab, which is the reason I am putting forth my wish for the additional forces with you, as my army is more acquainted to deal in that issue.”

King Rim and others get astound. Shamwill is busy in practicing with his sword and other martial arts as well. King Rim orders his attendant to call Shamwill in the imperial camp. Shamwill stops his practice and rushes to see the king. The minute Shamwill enters King Rim’s tent, King Rim addresses Shamwill, "He is the king of Shahr-e-Aab city from Persia and he wants us to know something which we are unaware of. I need you to be a part of it."

Shamwill nods his head. The king of Persia proceeds, "We have an extraordinary heap of sand lying a couple of miles away from the city, which comprises of sinkholes shrouded with sands on the ground. This coven of witches and warlocks who live there usually attack humans. And they take them away never to return. We named that land as Hooz-as-Sayah. So we avoid the place and put up signs of caution about the witches etc. all around the place to keep travelers and civilians away from danger."

Shamwill answers "Maybe, is that legend true"?

The Persian king answers "I believe in its authenticity. We have hammered four copper sacred nails plunged from the waters of paradise, given to us by God of Water. After long and continuous efforts of extraordinary supplication he showed up and we communicated our anxieties. Therefore this city is named after water on account of this reason. He gave us four copper nails of 10 meters each to hammer and sledge it on the four sides of the city so that they don't enter the Shahr-e-Aab. That maintains a strategic distance for them from entering the city. Yet, whoever they find outside the city, they don't leave any."

Everyone was worried about the untoward result they might have their way with faces dug in. Shamwill guarantees everybody that nothing will happen and that everybody will stay safe. Shamwill asks the Persian king, "Do they have any particular time?"

The Persian king answers, "No they don't, they can come whenever they wish, during the day or night." He requests King Rim to allow him to leave for the moment as he needs to take care of other arrangements. In this manner, the Persian king leaves from the camp. King Rim and Shamwill begin examining about the issue. King Rim speaks, "Shamwill, did you figure out how to take care of this issue of Shahr-e-Aab, or abandon them to endure?" Shamwill answers "No dear Majesty, my heart does not allow me to leave residents of Shahr-e-Aab in such troublesome circumstances. We need to search for a solution." King Rim says, "You are correct, Shamwill. Let's see how we can provide help in this matter."

Shamwill answers "If by chance you allow me, I want to investigate the matter closely." King Rim grants the authorization.

Shamwill sends a few soldiers to get the Persian priest to discuss the issue. The soldiers reaches the Persian priest and as requested by Shamwill, he agrees to come along with them. Persian priest pays a visit to the camp of Shamwill. Shamwill continues to wait for the priest fretfully. The priest enters the tent of Shamwill and addresses "yes dear Shamwill, is that anything I can help you with?"

Shamwill answers "Yes, King Rim and other royals have chosen to help Shahr-e-Aab and its dwellers. I have to know what made witches and warlocks to create havoc in Shahr-e-Aab and why have they picked this kingdom in particular." The Persian priest guarantees him that he will reveal everything about its beginning, as the King of Persia himself has disclosed it to them about the issue concerned.

He proceeds explaining to him "There lived a family in Shahr-e-Aab twenty years ago, that a family of two children. Their daughter was said to be among the loveliest teenagers of the city, one night, when the girl was working in her yard, some creature came flying, lifted her up and left towards the Hooz-as-Sayah. Her mother shouted and the whole of Shahr-e-Aab assembled. We reassured her that they would bring back their daughter and several men left for Hooz-as-Sayah, who also never returned.

We heard excruciating commotions of men shouting for help. Nobody could go there because of its dreadfulness. All chose to hold on until morning. During the day, thinking no mischief would happen, couple of men again left towards the Hooz-as-Sayah. We remained on higher planes of our kingdom watching them ride towards the Hooz-as-Sayah. The minute unicorns reached the ground of Hooz-as-Sayah, the ground opened up with sink holes and men vanished again with unicorns just like that.

The whole city was frightened with the imminent danger ahead and chose to remain inside their homes and began to fall short of food and sustenance, eventually leading to a few causalities. The King of Persia couldn't bear the torment of his people and chose to call all the priests from every corner of his kingdom. After all the holy priests assembled, they chose to supplicate and look for help from the God of water. During that period, people continue disappearing every day. Both men and women faced the wrath. One day, the girl who was taken away by the creature came to the city Shahr-e-Aab flying on a snake. Her mother ran and tried embracing her. But to her dismay, she was no more her daughter.

The mother got terrified watching the snake. She understood that her daughter had transformed into a witch. She requested that her family should accompany her for an incredible life. The mother rejected, and so did the whole family. At that point, she made the snake gulp all her family. It had eaten their fragile living flesh and tossed their bones on the people of Shahr-e-Aab.

Following a long supplication of day's together i.e.111 days, the God of Water appeared in the form of rain. The king and blessed priests disclosed to him the rage they are confronting. The God of Water had given these copper nails us to maintain a strategic distance from them coming inside the kingdom. At the point, when demanded by the King of Persia for the permanent solution of the problem, the God of Water answered, "Their numbers have surpassed every limit and people can't crush them. The king needs to demolish the Hooz-as-Sayah on a night without a moon, when they are extremely strong, with bolts dunked in stream water on their foreheads or hearts."

After that, the King of Persia had sent a few trained troops on a no moon night. However even they were not lucky enough to get back. As of now, we don't know how to overcome them as each endeavour has failed to destroy them. "Shamwill falls into profound thought. The holy priest allows Shamwill to take as much time as needed on this issue. Contemplating the disappointment of troops however, still he continues to work on the arrangements. Shamwill then chooses to visit the place personally. He requests the priest join him to King Rim for further discussion.

King Rim gets startled watching the priest and Shamwill come back together so early. He asks the reason from Shamwill. Shamwill uncovers the entire story of the Shahr-e-Aab. King Rim goes stunned. Shamwill puts forward his longing before the king by saying, "Dear King, I need to visit the place personally and especially on “no moon night” to see what the hell is going on in Hooz-as-Sayah.

King Rim answers "Shamwill, I would not prefer you to get in an unfortunate situation as you have other obligations too.”

Shamwill assures him, "Not to fret over it, I can keep myself safe for her. Just allow me to deal with this issue as I already know the issue.”

As nothing will work to stop Shamwill, King Rim grants him the permission. He requests that he take consent from his father as well. Shamwill goes with the priest to his father Gazualam and tells him the issue and seeks his permission.

Gazualam, after a long discussion, permits Shamwill to deal with the issue of Hooz-as-Sayah. Shamwill ventures out from his tent and addresses the Persian priest "Dear priest, I require some trustworthy soldiers who know about the place and who have great expertise in archery. The rest of the experts we have, will accompany with me in my main mission." The priest agrees and leaves.

The night has begun. And everyone is over stressed with the new and impending issue. As proposed by the Persian king, everyone takes their seats back in their camps which are restationed inside the city and special rooms are apportioned in the castle for the royals and nobles. Everyone goes to have some rest that night.

The morning takes after and all assemble on the tables of breakfast and begin to discuss the issue. Shamwill presents his arrangements before the kings. Gazualam, gets impressed, but he is equally worried about Shamwill's life.

Likewise, Shamwill proceeds, "It would comprise of 50 warriors, from whom 30 men will be from Shahr-e-Aab and the rest from my group of cavalries. 25 warriors will accompany me to the sinks of Hooz-as-Sayah. The rest will take their positions around the ground of Hooz-as-Sayah on “no moon night”."

King Rim answers, "So Shamwill, you are ready to give your head into a lion’s mouth?"

Shamwill answers, “If my god is with me, then nothing can bring any harm. I believe in myself and I need everyone to have faith in me." He then continues, "The rest who might stay outside on the ground will deal with the witches and warlocks who attempt to escape from the sink holes. They will be shot by arrows right away. We would make a special kind of container attached to the quiver which will comprise of river water and arrows ready to be utilized, each of which we will be tied to our backs. The holy priest and the rest can watch from the vintage points of the kingdom. We would light the entire territory with torches so that no malevolence escapes."

Gazualam states, "What would you do in sinkholes and how you will vanquish. I am extremely anxious about this.”

Shamwill answers "Kindly don't stress yourself, father, as I learnt everything from you. We would definitely succeed."

All bring glasses up together in cheers in the longing for achievement. The "no moon night" trails two long stretches of the day, so they choose to circumvent the city, watch the cultural activities and spend some great time at the royal residences. Subsequent to entering the markets, they see fascinating beauties chuckling and grinning towards Shamwill. The lanes adorned with articrafts, antique lamps, pots, and qgalyan.

Gazualam, the vizier of Egypt, and King Rim's commander-in-chief buys numerous things asked by the kings. At last, the night takes after and everybody assembles at a place in the market to have their fill. They stop over for the best eatery available in the city where chickens are broiled and meat of deer grilled. Everyone has soups, plates of mixed green leaves, deer steaks, chicken and so forth. After having these delicacies, they leave for the castle. After reaching there, the attendants inform all to assemble at the great hall as a special music event is organized by the nobles. The reason for the occasion was to showcase a special kind of music will be played from the stone which represents the famous art of Persia.

Everyone gets keen to witness such music that is to be played from stones. The guests are presented with special drinks. All get seated and the show starts. Two round rocks are set with a couple of little stones around it. The artists assemble, sit round, and begin playing the music.

Few more artists assemble and engage royal guests with their dancing art where they shake their bellies in accordance to the tune of the music. All show their amazement at the show's peculiarity and applaud the performers and the artists. After the occasion, all leave to rest in their chambers and that is how their second night is passed in Shahr-e-Aab. Lying on the bed, Shamwill recalls the time spent with Amunet when she use to sing and which made him lost in her charm.

He smiles at trivial things and at the same time getting lost in the magnificence of Amunet. Thinking about her, he embraces a cushion and falls asleep.

The day breaks and Shamwill integrates the cavalry and begins practicing his martial art. He also starts instructing them about the map of Hooz-as-Sayah. One night is left to launch an attack Hooz-as-Sayah. Vigorous training is given by the Shamwill to the cavalry. The king continues viewing the same from the balcony of the castle. Gazualam tells the kings, "Shamwill is exceptionally brave and dedicated. The individual whom I trust next after God in this world is just Shamwill".

King Rim answers "I agree, I feel something about Shamwill which is unexplainable."

Gazualam answers "I am not surprised in light of the fact that everybody feels so." All giggle and keep on talking. Gazualam asks the king, "for what reason did you leave your daughter and son-in-law in Egypt?" He answers, "Half a year, my daughter turns into a mermaid so she needs to live in water and on this journey, she can encounter many issues. Egypt has a major river, it supports the increase in the chances and agreeable for her survival."

The King of Persia states "I am sad, yet I truly don't comprehend what magical thing you are discussing. I never knew anything about such an event."

King Rim discloses to him the entire story of Cyrene city and the way Shamwill gets back his daughter from the Mermaid kingdom. Listening to it, the Persian king answers "My respect towards Shamwill has multiplied. He is an incredible warrior indeed." They turn their faces towards Shamwill again. At last the Persian king calls Shamwill to have his lunch and proceed with his training later.

Shamwill returns to his room and freshens up for lunch. He joins on the table along with the rest of the nobles. After lunch, he goes back to his training again. The Persian king announces the night as holy night and approaches the kingdom in order to pray to God for the entire night, as they are going to confront "no moon night" parallely where witches and warlocks gain powers to be extremely strong. Shamwill and others join the sacred ceremony during the evening. The Persian priest takes up the errands and recites from the blessed books and seek help from the God of water. After the night being prayed in supplication, each of them returns to their chamber to have some rest.

Before leaving, Shamwill tells each one of the warriors to prepare for the evening by themselves as a couple of arrangements must be dealt with personally for the "no moon night" which is around the same time. Evening takes after and Shamwill wakes up. He begins to prepare, recall his mother and appeals to god that in case that anything bad happens to him, god should take care of his mother. He has his breakfast and leaves towards the ground. He solicits one from the most courageous officers to get a woodworker. The best wood craftsman is presented before Shamwill. Shamwill guides him that he needs bolt bearers, which are 51 in number and could hold water.

The craftsman requests for some time until the nightfall, so that he gets the holder. He adds "It's a small work master, don't worry, I will get it done quickly."

Shamwill, in the end, requests the priest to get river water until the craftsman gets the holder. He pumps up water in big leather holders. The night falls and woodworker arrives with the bolt holders. He manufactures great holders in which a little glass like fragment is joined to the holder where river water can be filled with no spillage. Shamwill requests the priest to fill the water in it and allot it to all the chosen soldiers.

The priest take the holders into his temple and prepare the needed things. At that point, when the holy priest returns, Shamwill instructs him, "The minute you see the green flag, you should appeal to the God of Water for rain." The holy priest nods his head.

Consequently, the night falls and takes up its position. Shamwill and the soldiers march towards "Hooz-as-Sayah." They illuminate the place with torches (Fire) and sets respective soldiers all around the area. Shamwill and others start to hear odd shrieks from the ground. He disperses the soldiers as chosen and requests 25 warriors to accompany him in the sink holes.

He enters the ground of Sayah. The minute he ventures in, he hears the pit giving of strange noises. Shamwill declares to all "They have come to know about us. We must be ready and hustle just a bit as it's the only night we have." He gives an encouraging short speech to all. He shouts "follow me" and hops into the sink openings. The rest of the soldiers hop along with him. All skate in the sand sink holes which is followed by a tremendous passage. The sand takes every one of them underneath the ground. Flowingly which, they come down to the basement. Then they see warlocks flying towards them.

They get shocked by witnessing such people, some heading straight at them and some creeping on the walls and rooftops with wonderful mysterious powers of tossing fire balls at them. Shamwill eliminates a few of them.

The warriors likewise attack a few, but could hardly hurt them. Shamwill sees a few witches recounting spells on him and his warriors with alarming articulations. The minute Shamwill could understand anything, he and his men lose consciousness in a matter of seconds.

Hearing murmurs and giggles of witches which are so strange. Shamwill finds himself hung upside down surrounded by witches and warlocks with raging fire very close to his head underneath, and at the same time his men endure nobody can escape from. Shamwill asks "Who are you all? Free us then I will show you what we could do." No one answers him and they continue to whisper.

He sees a couple of warlocks and witches flying towards him on flying snakes. They approach Shamwill and stop. One of them tells "Such a great looking human, hardly found these days. I wish he was mine."

The other witch drives back and goes near Shamwill, She whispers, "I have not seen such deep grey eyes with such sparkling depth like an ocean."

She tries to caress Shamwill with sensuous touches. Shamwill yells at her, "Don't you dare touch me, you bloody witch. Make me free I will cut you in half."

The witch goes insane and begins to spin fast and stops suddenly. Brimming with outrage, she addresses Shamwill, "You don't recognize what our masters will do with you. You will lament for the day you came here." She flies back with her group with lot of fury. Shamwill in that condition looks around and finds one of the soldiers is missing.

He asks his companions, "Where is the other one?" nobody has the sure response. One of the warlock answers "one by one, we will take all of you and all of you have to taste death." All witches and warlocks leave the place with mischievous laughter.

Shamwill tries to free himself very hard and asks, "Where is our soldier? I don't understand why they took him and what they are doing with him now? Furthermore, why did that man say that they will take us one by one?"

Then one of the soldiers replies, "Master, May be they will use us for their witchcraft." Shamwill starts to think over the issue. In a while, he hears an uproarious sound of somebody coming towards the place.

Everybody's eyes go lifeless at seeing someone approaching them. He finds a similar group of witches and warlocks coming towards him. One of the witches grins at Shamwill. All stand in a line before Shamwill and his men. They all chuckle into commotion, Shamwill shuts his ears with his hands, and all bats from the hollows begin to fly towards the clamor. Bats in innumerable numbers fly towards the witches and warlocks. After passing through the soldiers, they hang themselves on the rooftop right beside Shamwill and his men welcoming their King of Warlocks and Witches. Witches and warlocks give a way and begin to fly back from their positions in the hollow places. Then a couple, who are extremely unnerving and look savage, enter the place.

The other witches addresses, "My dear king and queen of Hooz-as-Sayah, they are culprits who entered our premises and killed a few of our people."

The King of Sayah answers in a frightful voice "I know he made considerable progress. I can think about him since I am a warlock and see everything the minute I notice human. He came to erase us. He has no clue who we are."

And then the Queen of Sayah answers, “He is such a brave person to have come so far as nobody has done before, I would like to have his children in my womb” to which king reciprocates, “even I thought the same thing for you as you fantasize.”

Shamwill has no clue about what they are discussing. He tells, "I think you both have lost your mind." The king and queen snicker boisterously. Shamwill is shocked with the vulnerability. The king orders to set Shamwill free but to tie his hands and get him into the sacrosanct basement. The witches and warlocks fly and get him down, and ties his hands. Shamwill advises everybody not to lose hope, and assures them he will be back shortly to rescue all. They push Shamwill on the back of the snake and one warlock holds him as they leave towards the sacrosanct basement.

Every one of them starts to fear but the reason for moving ahead in the mission makes them hold their feelings. In the consecrated basement, Shamwill begins to free himself. The king asks his warrior witches and warlocks to tie him to a wooden bed. A unique course of action is made for the people in the sacrosanct basement for their coveted objectives. Shamwill continues his struggle to loosen himself, yet all endeavors go in vain.

Shamwill sets his eyes on what they are up to and soon he understands that this is their main process they carry out with individuals who they pick up from the city of Shahr-e-Aab.

The king starts to chant some spells and a seat is formed at a place for him on which he takes its position. The same is done by the queen. The other couple of orderly witches come near Shamwill and eject hello cells from his body, they place them in a flagon and place the cork tightly on that. He witness some vapours sprouting inside the flagon.

They places the flagons behind the wall racks of the room. The king states, "After some time when night gets darker in “no moon” the effect of cells will start, which would change into yolks in her body (that were injected in the female body). And in a couple of months, we will have strong and invincible warrior warlock and witches, as my queen can produce five children at one time. And once your hello cells are placed, we will follow the same process".

Shamwill is extremely wary of what is occurring at the place. The king order, "Get the hello cells from all the soldiers, so that we can have extraordinary warriors to vanquish this entire world.” He adds while walking towards the exit that, “Inject the hello cells in the body of a women whom we have picked up from the Shahr-e-Aab".

All leave the place cheerfully. Shamwill begins thinking profoundly about what must be his next step. His mind gives him few solutions, and with a grin, he tries setting his hands free. Yet, after making couple of decent attempts, he can't untie the rope. He sees that the queen is walking towards him. He prevents his body from moving and shaking. The queen comes and sits close to Shamwill and utters in his ears, "My dear brave man, thc minute I saw you I had fallen in love with you and your bravery. I want you to be mine. I am prepared to leave this place for you. Indeed, I am the same teenager who was picked from the streets of Shahr-e-Aab, and had been converted to a monstrous witch by the king".

Shamwill watches her intently. He discovers vapours and smoke coming from her ears and eyes. In a flash, Shamwill abstains from looking into her eyes. He answers, "I owe my life to another female and I love her deeply. My affection isn't contingent like yours."

She gets irate but remains calm and composed at her place. She answers, "Alright, what If I set you free and prove my love?"

Shamwill answers, "Without any doubt, still you will not get me. But if you want you can save this world from a fury of witches and warlocks."

She answers, "I don't care about this world. However, as my heart is a piece of human body, I am obliged to it. I was a decent human like you, but predetermination played with me and very soon I will be a completely turned into witch as a whole, by heart and soul."

Shamwill asks "Why is that so?"

The queen answers "This is on the grounds what king wants me to transform completely without being left with any human trace and he will do it beyond any doubt."

Shamwill begins thinking cautiously and asks the queen, "Would you be able to do one great deed before you turn into all evil?" The heart of queen, which is still human somewhat, begins to change and she answers, "Yes, I can, I am capable of it."

Shamwill advises her "So unfasten me, so that I can leave this place with my soldiers without hurting anybody."

She thinks hard about it and agrees. She answers, "Ok, I will release you after the process of tonight's activity of rituals that are concerned with the injection of hello cells and when the hello cells are infused in my body, I will come to unfasten you."

Shamwill thanks the queen and still, his mind is loaded with questions. Noticing him, the queen asks, "What are you thinking now?" Shamwill answers, "Despite everything still I don't see how somebody can make a soul and body? It is only the creator who can do such a thing." The queen answers "The king is eternal on earth as he was a servant at heaven in the chamber of souls. After knowing the procedure of making a life, he escaped from heaven and arrived here."

It's new point of amazement for Shamwill. He says "Is it real? I can't believe this."

The queen answers "Yes, it is true, the females which are picked from the road are just a piece of production machines and men are utilized for extraction of "hello cells" and consolidated in the vapours of spell."

Verily, she gasps heavily. Shamwill needs to find out in detail and subsequently, interest for the same develops in him. He continues to pester her more. He asks, "Still, I don't understand one thing, that how a soul is formed?

The queen answers, "The process of making a soul is not a simple one.” It's a painstaking process beyond any doubt. A “hello cell” comprises of an erosion of light which is alive for a period of time in warm atmosphere. Thus, the spell keeps it warm as same as a womb does. What's more, at the right moment, it is injected in the female's' body as the vapours changes its nature from human to witch. At that point, the womb of the female body is like a carafe where something just develops.”

Shamwill asks, "Then how many more are in process? Then, what is the end result for people who are picked from the city of Shahr-e-Aab?" The queen answers, “Just once, the male and female are utilized for delivering 5 witches soon after that, the levels of vitality drop down and therefore they are sent back to the creation."

Shamwill gets a little frightened about the strategy as they have extracted his hello cells as well. The queen looks towards Shamwill and says, "You don't have to worry as I don't want you to die and beyond any doubt I will help you in getting out from here."

Shamwill still needs to have some more information about Hooz-as-Sayah. He continues with his next question, "You said in regard to sending back to the creation? How could that be? You mean executing it?" The queen answers, "No, it's not simply killing but rather making another factor to which human race will end and just witches and warlocks remain to run the show. I know it's troublesome for you to know about such a thing. But, let me disclose you in detail." Shamwill nods his head restlessly and the queen proceeds, "A hello cell comprises of a small erosion of light appended to a living cell and wavelength which a human can't see as human eyes are not capable of watching it. Rather it's told that couple of creatures do have that power of sensing and witnessing the light which enters and leaves the body. This is then framed in existence with vitality and strong wavelength. That is the reason when a human dies, nobody can see that light and wavelength which leaves the body. That is the means by which the process is carried out in heaven. However, to make witches just an additional stage is added where the spells are combined with "hello cells" in the flask.

People are used for once and then they are burnt, boiled and then buried in the outskirts of Shahr-e-Aab. When their soul leave the body, it finishes the journey of this life, where it has been as good or evil on demise of the one's deeds. Good soul is a white light and bad is either red or yellow. Nowadays, we hardly experience such good souls. The good soul joins the star. A star is nothing but a cluster of a millions of good souls which are white in color, which involves positive vitality. Thus, the number of witches that die will join the sun resulting in getting hotter and hotter, leading in the triumph over the king of witches and warlocks."

Shamwill tosses an instant question "Shouldn't we missing something about evil souls?"

The queen answers with a grin, "It joins sun as comprehended, that's why sun is yellow and red which is only negative vitality. This thing will add one day in destroying human race with its hot nature."

Shamwill goes stunned. He asks the queen, "Is it a similar process carried out in heaven?" the queen answers "Maybe or maybe not."

Shamwill tosses another dice for his information "Wouldn't we be able to stop the king?"

The queen answers "Only gods have the capacity and know the answer for it. As far as I know, I have been instructed to be away from extreme fire and few drops of water too which can be dangerous to me and my people."

Shamwill recalls and comprehends that the God of Water has officially given him the solution for this issue and not following the way in which it has to be, was the reason for the failure before.

Shamwill reveals that he needs to leave before any issue emerges. The queen agrees and takes a gander at Shamwill with adoration and tears. Accepting the fact that after betraying the king, she would barley be alive, she leaves from the place to come back again after the placement process. There over the surface of the basement soldiers continue attempting to unfasten the ropes while the witches and warlocks continue to laugh at their failures.

With such a huge level of anger on the faces, the soldiers converse with each other. One soldier says "Be calm and wait till Shamwill returns."

The other soldier asks, "When will he return? To what extent we should hold on?" The soldier replies, "Hold on until he comes back, he will be back to rescue us and if by chance if you still attempt to unfasten your hands, you will fall in flame which is burning right below you."

All fighters resume. In the middle of the night, all soldiers suspending in the air hears a chuckling sound made by warlocks and witches for the procedure that have begun.

The same thing follows with Shamwill too. He gets startled to hear such voices but he comes to know finally.

Shamwill takes sigh of relief that the queen will be arriving soon. After some time, the day is about to break, he witnesses the queen in the sacrosanct basement. She feels love for Shamwill which she expresses through her eyes. She comes close to Shamwill and tells him "You leave this place as quickly as time permits as the sinkholes tend to shrink during the day as no one from outside can come in and go out without consent of the king."

Shamwill pretends that he is leaving before the queen. The queen leaves from the place likewise.

But like planned, he just comes back from a window of a basement. He sets fire in the consecrated basement to destroy all the hello cells and flagons. Indeed, even the cells which they removed from Shamwill get decimated.

He scales towards his soldiers and kills the evil watchers. He tosses his mysterious rope, which he won in the devour by King Rim, to the opposite sides and orders them to cut their tied ropes from the suspended state and catch the rope which he has tossed. The specialty of this rope is that it need not be tied with anything or to any support, it has its grasp at any place and is noticeable to everyone. He orders all of them to hold the rope, creep on it and get to the opposite side without falling in flame. All the soldiers follow the instruction and move towards the opposite side. The fire from the basement, which was set by Shamwill begins expanding. All the warlocks and witches start flying aimlessly around their homes, which are in the form of massive nests. The moment they encounter Shamwill and his group they choose to attack.

Shamwill shouts at everyone to follow same method of killing. All the soldiers raise their arches and arrows to shoot at them (In their chests and head). All the warlocks and witches continue to die. With this massacre, Shamwill moves towards the exit. One of the soldiers then asks Shamwill, "Why are we going out? For what reason we are not killing everyone present here?"

Shamwill answers, "The sink holes will shrink in few minutes and we can't go out after some time resulting in death, so its better we go out and do things which we planned." The soldier nods his head. With mass killing, they make it towards the sink holes. Crawling out from the sink holes, they come out and get themselves to a safer side of Hooz-as-Sayah. The soldiers who are on the ground above, hurry to help Shamwill and others. Shamwill turns towards them and orders them to take their positions. He then sends a few to get some ground oil as part of their plan. Within a few minutes, the soldiers bring great quantity of ground oil.

Shamwill requests everyone to pour the oil in the sink holes. All the oil containers are poured in the sink holes as instructed. Few of the witches and warlocks originate from the sink holes. Shamwill begins to shoot at them with archers. At last Shamwill sets everything on fire. The entire Hooz-as-Sayah is burnt and destroyed.

Inside the sink holes of Hooz-as-Sayah, the king of warlocks and witches, hear pitiable shrieks and wails of his people. In a second, he close his eyes and with his intuitive power envision everything that has happened. He gets up in outrage and leaves from his nest. With heaps of outrage and with the feeling of being betrayed by his own, he looks around and finds the queen standing to the opposite side of his sacred nest.

In a minute before he could tell anything to her, she hops into the water pond and lets herself to get burnt. The king grins as she punished herself. He rushes to save his populace. Within a moment, he sees an enormous fire emerging from the sacrosanct basement (Below) and furthermore from the sink holes (above). He takes his ride on a flying snake, which is tied outside his nest. He sees everything getting demolished and flares up to one of the sink holes which is secretive.

Alongside, Shamwill and officers continue to pour oil until the point where the entire ground is burnt into ashes, leaving a single massive hole in the ground.

Shamwill requests the soldiers to show green flag to the holy priest. Keeping in mind that fire and water both can be dangerous for Hooz as Sayah Shamwill uses this trick. Obeying to him, the soldier shows the green flag. The holy priest appeals the God of Water and therefore the rain begins. The entire downpour tops off the sink holes of Hooz-as-Sayah. The rest of the warlocks and witches get annihilated with the rain water which acts like a corrosive on them. The king of witches and warlocks escapes from the place. Thinking everyone is dead, Shamwill and his warrior leaves the place too. Shamwill reaches the city where everyone celebrates. The king of Persia pays thanks to Shamwill for his bravery.

The minute Shamwill reaches his chamber to rest, he hears people screaming all over the city. Every one of the royals and nobles surges towards the corridor. They finds huge fire balls being tossed from the sky on Shahr e Aab. Shamwill keeps running towards the pinnacle to see the issue. After reaching on the tower of the palace, he sees that the king of warlocks and witches is alive and carried by his flying snake which is brimming with anger through its eyes, tossing fire balls from its tongue on Shahr-e-Aab.

Shamwill shoots arrows, but to his surprise nothing effects the chaperon of heaven as everlasting mortality was allowed to him by the creator. Shamwill decides to ask the Persian holy priest.

He asks the holy priest to provide with a solution to defeat the God of Water and request to god to appear. The holy priest begins supplicating and within no time, the God of Water shows up. Shamwill surges towards him and requests for a solution. The God of Water answers, "I can battle him out as we both are immortals. Yet, beyond any doubt, he will destroy Shahr-e-Aab." The King of Persia asks “What we are supposed to do now?" The God of water replies, “You need to gather people as much as you can and vacate this place, as per the circumstances." The King of Persia fills with desolation and tears.

At last he agrees watching no hope for the situation. Shamwill, army and residents of the city begins the rescue process and they take everybody from a concealed route into the forest area. The fight starts between the God of Water with the king of witches and warlocks in the air. Every deserted citizen watches the battle from the forest. With the fireballs falling all over, the whole city begins transforming into ashes. Verily, morning gazes. The God of water prays to the creator for help. Following which, few angels descend from the sky who capture the king of witches and take him back to the layers of the sky. The God of Water takes a gander at the city which transformed into ashes due to fire balls leading so many people burnt into ashes which makes him sad with no solution. He chooses to bury the dead to rest in peace. With his power, everybody gets automatically buried in their respective graves through his godly power, without any effort being made. The Persian king states to God of Water with anguish and tears, "My Lord, my people are dead and the whole city has been annihilated, and from Shahr-e-Ab, which is the city of water, it has changed to Shahr-e-khakister which is city of the burnt." He then turns up towards his people and announces with pain, "I pronounce this city as Shahr-e-khakister, and it will be known by this name from now onwards."

This way, all leave with great agony to other part of kingdom.

Passing through the wildernesses with camels, unicorns and the remaining stuff with them, the army, the residents and the nobles' venture out on a great journey to another side of the kingdom. The Persian king and the other nobles walk along with torment and distress. Shamwill and different royals reassure the King of Persia and guarantees for a better city and a better kingdom in future. Shamwill, King Rim and other nobles with a state of agony take last farewells. Abruptly, the King of Persia asks everyone to hold on for a minute. King Rim and Shamwill take a halt. The King of Persia solicits all the people from Shahr e Aab to proceed with their journey towards Persian city where they are heading to. The other respectable men of Persia without soliciting anything, oblige the order given by the king of Persia. Shamwill tries getting some information about the sudden change in his plans.The King of Persia says, "I cannot go to my people empty handed. I need to develop and extend my domain and I can't come back to city with no assets. Thus, I planned to proceed with my journey until the point, where I can locate renounceable resources to overcome the losses as we lost lots of valuable resources and assets in Shahr-e-Khakister."

The army begins to march as per their mission. King Rim turns his head towards Gazualam and asserts, "It's very disappointing that we could not save Shahr-e-Aab."

Gazualam answers "I can't trust my eyes that what had occurred."

Shamwill adds "The King of Persia is extremely strong and he will reconstruct his empire at any cost now and may be much better this time. They are free from evil wrath and can live with no fear now."

Gazualam gestures his head in acknowledgment of the statement. They all keep on traveling for the day. They rest during evenings and proceed with their journey during the day. Days continue to pass and they cross the outskirts of Persia and step in Turkmenistan.

Chapter Seventeen

Mystery of Bamiyan Mountains

There, all nobles decide to break the monotony and rest for all day & night. During the night, the Persian king addresses all, "My friends, from here, I would take up my journey with my cavalry towards my goal and with an objective to search resources and better place for my people. I wish all of you a good fortune for your mission. I am thankful to all of you who had helped me and my kingdom from a dreadful future wrath. I take everything positively now as it would have put an end to numerous kingdoms, even to this entire world.

I would be starting my journey from the very next morning towards Uzbekistan, as I heard through some sailors that after Uzbekistan, there are resources and fertile lands which could help my people in rebuilding a better kingdom." All raise toast and applaud for the Persian king. Shamwill pays tributes the dead dwellers (civilians) of Shahr-e-Khakister.

The morning takes after and the Persian king torts with his procession towards Uzbekistan. Later, as heard the king defeated Kazakhstan and settled in the delightful city of Mouru, which is now called Marv. He had defeated numerous cities of Uzbekistan and extends his realm.

Later city Mouru turns into the capital of Persia from where all exchange of resources takes place to different areas of the kingdom that is ruled by Persian king. Shamwill's great zeal and war with witches and warlocks had always remained in some part of his memories. He states to Shamwill that if needed he will always be on his side in his mission and join him soon. In this manner his relationship with Shamwill turns out to be inseparable.

After Resting as decided the nobles and army charges up for their journey. They begin to start again with their journey. The journey continues with its demands. Every day's practice and meditation keeps Shamwill well-oriented towards his mission. King Rim and Gazualam considers the entire situation for the betterment of humanity in saving this world and its human race.

"On the continuous," back to back "journey" they enter the border of Afghanistan and as sunset falls they set their camps in one of the Bamiyan mountain ranges. Verily, they feel cool breeze from behind the mountains with which all begin shivering because of cold. Gazualam addresses "what is there all the time at every place we stop! I am not ready for any surprise now." They move forward to see the matter behind the sudden change in the climate. Shamwill sends Ouzo to hover and he continues to check. Ouzo takes his flight and in minutes he comes back.

He comes back to Shamwill and tells that he cannot see anything due to fog and clouds surrounding the mountains. Shamwill stops everyone and tells "all you step back as we are almost into night it's and getting dark. It's not safe at this time, we will check the place tomorrow morning." All the soldiers step back and move towards their tents. King rim and Gazualam gets inside their tents due to extreme cold. Soldiers set some bonfire and rest activities continues. All nobles begun to come out of their camps after some time and warm their hands on bonfire. The royal cooks prepare food and soups for the nobles. Shamwill joins at bonfire. While conversing he feels someone watching him and as he turns back he finds no one around. Gazualam asks Shamwill "what happened?" He replies "I felt someone's presence behind me, might be my illusion and suspicion." Then he neglects about it and continues to talk. They all rest in and outside the camps. Suddenly they all hear sound of clouds that are creating noisy thunder. All rush to make arrangements thinking it will rain. The thunder starts making loud noise over the ground and mountains.

All gets frightened thinking where they can escape and hide from it, as they find nothing close by apart of the same mountain range. The king rim, Shamwill, vizier of Egypt and Gazualam starts rushing and orders the soldiers to pack off the camps and hurry further to the buckle of the mountains. Soldiers pack their stuff and hurry towards the mountain range. With horses, chariots, camels etc. they start trotting. Suddenly to the surprise of all, clouds starts separating from each other which disperse to move separately. Each cloud starts following each of the soldier like an umbrella (they were mysterious).

The cloud abducts the soldier in a moment and the soldiers, one by one start vanishing. Watching the whole scenario Shamwill screams, "All of you stop!" A thought erupts in his mind that how a cloud can hold a unicorn, when compared to men who are very lighter than unicorns. He adds, "Get down and take cover below your unicorns." They obey his orders.

Therefore, clouds somehow halts. As far as Shamwill could see its dark and grey with clouds. Surprisingly, each cloud seems to behave like living beings. They stop, move and communicate with each other making thunderous sounds.
The vizier of Egypt takes out a stick which contains enchanted sand of Egypt. He removes the head of the stick and blows some sand around. All area becomes very quiet as though someone has comprehend something.
In a moment, it starts raining heavily and in no time the clouds melts in the form of rain and the sky gets clear. Shamwill and other get surprised with the incident. Following to it, a cool breeze starts blowing and gradually begins to blow fast. After a while wind vigorously blowing dries each and everything i.e. their clothes, animals and carriages. Gazualam asks the troop, "What has actually happened?" king rim replies "don't think about what had happened, check where we reached now". All see that they reached at a place or can be said clouds got them to the center of the ground of the mountain range which consists of multiple lakes. Deep blue water just like crystals shining in the sky, the purity of water can make any human fell in love with its each drop.
There, they see moon light on that area is instilling life and some special attention for the place. The place looks so stunning and twinkling that everyone loses all sense of direction in its excellence. Shamwill cannot stops himself in praising the place and therefore he begins admiring.
"The diamonds scattered on the mount,
Like a queen wearing the crown
Like a heaven is scattered on the ground
Like a peacock opened its feathers
Little shady and little brighter near together.

Verily, Gazualam keeps his hand on Shamwill's shoulder. Shamwill stops and looks at him. The king rim keeps moving around and inspects the place. Gazualam states "what might be the reason for someone to bring us here. And who might be the one". The vizier of Egypt says "hope we don't face more surprises." Suddenly earth starts shaking, horses and camels start tumbling.

Shamwill orders the army to be prepared. All see a soft light emitting from the lakes and the water gushing out from it. Progressively, water touching the sky as its flowing from the ground or flowing from the sky. They see all lakes gushing and emitting light. Shamwill count the lakes and finds it to be seven in number. Air gets filled up with the scent of jasmine flower. The smell raises sense in a feeling of something pious and pure. Gazualam states that, "take positions and raise your weapons". Earth starts shaking more and soldiers begin to fall and nobles try balancing themselves on horses, chariots and camels out of fear of falling down.

Following that, they see the volume of light has increased and like a fast light just travelled from the depth of the lake. There they see excellent fairies appearing noticeably all around setting their eyes on with the smiles. Everyone just cannot blink watching their beauty. Shamwill does not show much interest for them and raises a question that, "we were on our journey. There was no need for you to behave with us like this. What do you want from us?" the one seems to be higher in their rank. The head of the fairy replies, "This horizon belongs to the God and we protect it and live here. It's known by name "Egress Empyrean", we hardly find any men passing by from this region. There are only few places on planet which are close and connected to heaven and hell.

This place is conspicuous and prominent one. All travelers know that this water is not used for drinking and there is no well close by. What got you here? The other fairy adds, "With so many people?" Shamwill answers "we are going on a mission to rescue someone who is very dear and also to save the world eventually." Listening to him the fairy that is actually in red colour attire as when compared to who are in white & blue makes her stand apart and she replies, "humans! I don't think humans have so much of power." King rim replies "I am the king of Cyrene city and we have conquered many kingdoms and beheaded many evil entities.

You better not tell us." Gazualam stops king rim from getting on his nerves. Shamwill asks "now tell us why we are here, I told you the reason so shall we leave?" the fairy replies "you are free and as you have answered us honestly we can give you this place for you to use". Shamwill refuses. The red fairy insists Shamwill to forgive her and accept her apology as she made them suffer and created obstacles'. The red fairy replies to Shamwill "I am Red Fairy, called as God of Red too and I am the prominent of all fairies. Everything red in nature is created by me. I really like your brave attitude but I am bound to my duties. When I had smelt the sand of Egypt I came to know that the people who stepped down here are from the land of Priests. So I stopped creating any obstacles for you all. Now it's your desire if you want to live here or to leave." Gazualam addresses the fairies "as you said this water cannot be consumed so what we should wait here for?" the fairy replies, "Until the time you live here I will make this water consumable with my mystical powers." King rim agrees with no other option as they are very tired and don't want to travel further. The red fairy creates 40 crystal aputiak (igloo) with her magic wand. All nobles and army bow their heads in gratitude to the fairies. The fairies get back to the lake. Shamwill and royals take their accord. Morning gazes and Shamwill comes out of her aputiak, he is simply awed with the beauty of “Egress Empyrean”. He comes out and feels the cool breeze of the mountains. Though wearing overcoats made of heavy fur they cannot resists their teeth chattering. Shamwill finds Gazualam standing outside prior to him. He keeps his hand on the shoulder of Gazualam and asks him “Why did you wake up so early. Usually you sleep for long time. Don’t You? He deduces, “I feel you dint sleep all night. What’s the matter?” Gazualam turns towards him and asks Shamwill with a questionable face, “You know I am disturbed from what transpired last night. It should not have happened.” Shamwill replies “yes I know the way red fairy has troubled us.” Gazualam replies, “Don’t you remember anything?” Shamwill replies, “We were sleeping all night. Weren’t we? Why u are acting like something untoward occurred?” What happened to you?” Gazualam is about to remind Shamwill about the last night’s incident where suddenly, the king rim addresses from behind, “That was fun. I was very tired and fell asleep soon after”. Shamwill looks at Gazualam with an interrogative manner. Gazualam hides his expressions and laughs at it and continues to talk about different things.

The King rim orders the army to get ready and pack their stuffs. Army gets themselves occupied with work. Shamwill feels something painful in his neck. He gets near the lake to check what had happened. He finds a small wound and realizes he had fallen off something during rest. He neglects and starts thinking about Amunet. He smiles and assumes reflections of Amunet in water and suddenly he sees one illustrious soft hand in water. He pulls the hand towards him and takes her out. To his surprise he sees a red fairy in it.

To his surprise he didn't anticipate and expect her. She comes out and tells Shamwill "Don't be scared. I came to give you final goodbyes for your mission." Shamwill smiles at her in acceptance of her statement. Gazualam keeps looking around what that was happening. Red fairy soars and comes towards Gazualam and tells something softly in his ears. The face of Gazualam turns pale hearing to it. King rim looks at Gazualam with surprise. The fairy address king rim and vizier of Egypt and wishes them good luck. She flies back in the lake and disappears.

All pack their luggages and set out on camels, chariots, unicorns and carriages. All take up their rides and leave the place of "Egress Empyrean". Travelling far long an extended period towards their mission, they cross valleys, rivers and steep mountains followed by many night. They set up camps as usual and start with daily activities. Shamwill keeps watching Gazualam who is lost in his thoughts. He tries talking to Gazualam but somebody or the other keeps interrupting them. During the journey and facing its challenges Shamwill forgets and ignores the miserable face of Gazualam. However they tend to focus on the rescue of Amunet. Passing through Afghanistan they reach to a place called "Tajikistan". Trotting at day and resting at night makes all restless.

The curiosity for Shamwill keeps on increasing day by day. On the other hand king rim starts noticing Gazualam and his conduct which had changed drastically. One day he wishes to ask Gazualam the reason for being quiet. Gazualam doesn't state any reason and tries pretending as if nothing has happened. The king rim does not agree and leaves.

Chapter Eighteen

The Tortoise Island

Few days pass by and they cross the borders of "Tajikistan". King rim notices again Gazualam getting depressed as he approaches Gazualam and asks him again. Gazualam could not resist the secrecy of "egress empyrean" and discloses it to the king Rim.

Shamwill gets busy in his martial arts and he glances on Gazualam and King Rim, watching their pale faces he cannot stop himself and he rushes towards them. He approaches them and asks "what is the matter father as I am watching you since we have passed "egress" u seems to be worried." Gazualam could not utter even single word and king rim behaves like he has some other work and he signs off. Gazualam decides in his mind that it is not the right time to tell Shamwill about it. Therefore he behaves normal and replies to him, "Shamwill I am worried about you. And as we are getting close to our goal. I fear for your life."

Shamwill assures that nothing will happen and everything will be alright at the end. Gazualam nods his head and leaves from the place to look after preparations. Shamwill looks at sky and looks around with deep sighs. All gather for lunch. King rim asks his attendants to crack some jokes so that they have some good time. King rim requests Gazualam to act normal as all the reason of rescue could be affected by it. Gazualam takes deep sighs. Therefore they continue their travelling towards the place called “Peking”, which falls on the way towards “Mount Mummit”. Finally, the army and nobles reach the borders of “Tajikistan” and enter “Peking”.

They witness large number of monks passing by and continues to observe them for a while. They feel peace with the ambience around. Finally, they enter the capital city of “Peking”, a few soldiers stop the army and enquire the purpose of their visit in such considerable number. As the messenger is now sent by vizier of Egypt to the king of “Peking”, the messenger comes back to the army in no time. He shows the letter of acceptance with a royal stamp of the king to the soldiers of “Peking”. The soldiers allow all to pass by the country. As Peking is a vast kingdom the army has to take long journey. Passing through multiple villages and cities they prepare to rest during night and travel the whole day.

From the hotter equatorial lines they enter to the northern hemispheres of the country. The cold climate of the region creates challenges to them yet no one seems to lose hope. They keep travelling and hot soups help them cut off the cold. During the journey Gazualam’s restlessness grows and his sleeps gets occupied with thoughts. King rim keeps staring Shamwill with the secret that is shared by Gazualam with him. Shamwill keeps on asking but Gazualam and king Rim keeps on distracting his mind with something or the other. While riding towards their destination they see a huge tortoise structure from a distance and Shamwill torts his horse further for few miles going faster towards it.

He starts screaming out of joy, as it’s mentioned in the riddle about it. He screams, “We have found the tortoise land”. Watching Shamwill so happy, Gazualam and King Rim speeds their unicorns and reach to the place of

Shamwill. They also express their happiness and closeness to the goal. They tort fast to see the land of tortoise. They go closer and closer to the land. All of them feel humidity in air, in the form of steam.

Vizier of Egypt stops everyone and tells, “I think there is water or ice before the land, we need to slow down and watch our steps. All march slowly and evening falls off. They reach in front of the land and they find it as island surrounded by water & ice but the neck of the tortoise land seems to be missing. All of them, spend their night close to the island. Shamwill just keep on thinking throughout the night, to cross the water body and hence he decides to use the wooden pontoons or log rafts. With couple of soldiers he works hard until midnight. Shamwill keeps watching the island restlessly during he makes the log rafts.

After a restless night Shamwill falls asleep for some time. He wakes up when one of the soldiers calls him up and states, “Master sun is about to rise. The army is ready for the further journey.” Listening to it Shamwill wakes up and gets fresh to march. All tort towards the island. They find an unusual water body, where water is flowing in the opposite direction. Astonishingly they begin to watch and discuss how to sail on such water. In a moment, Shamwill gets on the log rafts without even thinking for a second. He announces all to follow him. He pushes the water in the opposite direction of waves therefore it becomes easy for all. Here the trick played by Shamwill works finely. Sailing towards the tortoise island, they witness the island surrounded with waterfalls and heavy fog. The waterfall which is flowing from earth towards the mountains and fog emerging from the ground towards the sky, makes it look spooky. The cool breeze is enjoyed by all the army. As it’s the longest of any journeys they had been through, they reach the coast of the island. All step down from the rafts and begins to walk towards the island. All of them keep watching around keenly.

Shamwill, King Rim and Gazualam praise the place, the moment, they step down from the rafts. King rim says "I find this place unusual of all, because of such beautiful nature and feeling of joy which is giving me positive vibes to my persona. I expect things to be better than before." Lost in the beauty of Tortoise Island, Gazualam forgets about the dark truth that he is carrying with him from "Egress Empyrean".

All of them march and enter the island. After walking for about 50 yards, they feel sand as dry as it does not belong to the shore. The sand seems to move and rustle is being heard. The sand from the shore starts moving, with this they all get frightened and moves back, without noticing that the sand is rolling on their boots in upward direction on their body.(Of all the army). The sand rolls all over the body and tickle everyone's ears, feet and stomach. All get amused with the act that takes place. The army starts laughing, giggling and jumps from one side to the other. In a while the sand stops and falls off on the ground. Everything seems to get back to normal.

After walking for more 20 yards, they find beautiful purple pebbles overlaid in a line of the shore. Gazualam states, "What a beautiful and unique stones this island has and therefore, he picks one of the pebble. In a moment, the pebble showers some water on the face of Gazualam and closes back again. Gazualam, throws off the pebble and asserts, "I just got petrified." Shamwill adds, "Beauty is the sign of jeopardy and the more beautiful it becomes it turns out to be dicey." Vizier of Egypt adds, "Hmm" and they continue to walk further.

They witness the ground of island scaly just like tortoise skin. They begin to watch their steps carefully. Suddenly, all hear a sound, “ouch”! Everyone sees here and there. They look around and see sweet little herbs filled with life and with the ability to talk. The soldiers step out from the herbs. Shamwill bends down to see such amazing miracle of nature. He questions, “Little plant how you can talk?” the plant replies, “we are not supposed to talk to strangers. “Oops” and then the plant stops talking. Shamwill addresses everyone, “as we have come so far and encountered mystical journey, so don’t expect things to be peaceful further.” All nods their heads.

Shamwill commands everyone that, “hang on, as it could be a sign of danger too”.

However not being afraid of anything they continue to move forward. While walking inside the island they encounter dense forest, which consists of just 3 feet short trees and bushes.

The most pleasant part is that one could see the other side of the forest which has small range of Ghats. King rim finds Shamwill worried and addresses Shamwill, “This seems to be simple and easy. What are you worried about?” Shamwill replies, “As we can see the other side but we don’t know what is underlying these trees as forest seems to be so dense and everything has life here. This island is new to us and have unusual things on it. Therefore I am worried about the forest mysteries.” King rim comforts Shamwill and encourages him to face the situation.

Therefore all move ahead towards the forest. Incredulous plants and trees move and make alley wherever they stride. They find all types of trees behaving similar to mankind. The army turns up towards the nobles and beseech for a solution. Shamwill assures them that nothing will happen and all will remain safe. Shamwill asks everyone to be alert and be careful. Hence, they continue to walk forward. With the trees moving and army marching in the forests, the soldiers express their feelings about fresh cold breeze which is revitalizing their senses. Passing out from the forest, the army and nobles reach finally to the other side of the region.

They find Ghats unconnected to the other side of the land. Shamwill realizes that, it's the end of the island and the neck of the tortoise is missing which is connecting one side to the other. He heads to see if any solution can be found to the issue.

The army rest on the elevated Ghats, thinking how to cross the island. The vizier of Egypt astonishingly watches a tomb like structure on which a tree has grown. He instantly brings up to the notice of all nobles and approaches the tomb.

They witness a grave from which a green tree has emerged. Everyone gets around the grave watching who might be the one.

Verily, earth shakes and a saint from the grave appears and stands in front of all. The saint has the same tree as part of his head which was watching all. The saint has half dusky and half white looks with leaves and branches as his head and hair. He addresses the army that, "who are you all and why you want to cross this island. Don't you know the way is hazardous?" Shamwill takes the initiative to answer the saint and replies, "we want to cross this island and reach the "Mount Mummit." Saint tree replies, "Do you know the meaning of 'Mummit'?" Shamwill replies "No". The saint tree answers, "it's called the "Mountain of Dead". I suggest you not to go there with such a big army." Shamwill replies, "Dear saint tree, we all are here to save someone who is very close to us and also to save this world from a future wrath." The saint tree agrees as his duty is just to warn. The tree from his head grows longer and stronger resulting in integrating the two sides, acting like a bridge.

The army pays tributes to the saint tree and leaves towards the bridge. All begin to cross the bridge, when they are about to reach the other side, the massive hippos from water appear and shake the bridge. Watching it, Shamwill woes that, "the place has started showing its deadliness." Few men get killed by massive hippos. They mourn and continue to move further.

Chapter Nineteen

Discovery of Mount Mummit (The Mountain of death)

After crossing the tortoise island, which connects to the range of mountains leading to "Mount Mummit", they land at the open barren ground which has dead bushes and elongated by steeply mountains all around. The army marches further. They realizes that, dry and dead bushes are followed by green and lively bushes with dense forests, valleys and steeply mountains. They walk deep down for hours and then King Rim states to vizier of Egypt and Gazualam that, "we are going to end up walking long in this way, therefore we need to check and cut down the use of resources." As Shamwill is busy in leading army, vizier of Egypt calls out Shamwill for a small break. They set food on the tables and serve themselves. During their break vizier of Egypt discloses the input given by king rim in front of all. Shamwill replies, "We have limited sources and we cannot carry all our men on it." King rim replies "the moment of the fact is that, we need to reach the "Mount Mummit" as soon as we can and the army will march towards the mountain range to where we can check the current situation of our sources." Gazualam adds, "Yes, we have flying carpets, other mystical powers, ouzo will lead us and the army too." Shamwill agrees and decides to work on the given inputs. A detail discussion is carried out with all officials. They plans the journey that has to be lead further. Shamwill asks everyone to make quick arrangements, the moment he is back from the discussion.

Therefore, Shamwill takes ouzo, flying carpet and asks everyone to hold at their places as he will patrol the place and come back soon. Shamwill takes his flight in the sky on his flying carpet with ouzo. He sees the place up to a few kilo meters and finds very long stretch of mountains. Ouzo tries taking him very far but to reach back to the army, he return back with ouzo. After coming back to the army, he informs them about his surveillance. King rim states that, "for sure "Mount Mummit" is still far and we need to continue our journey." The army sets up and march towards the direction showed by ouzo. The chilling nights and days do not break determination of any one. As the land has dense forest they hunt and feed themselves. After a long journey of one week, including seven days and six nights again Shamwill gets on his flying carpet and takes the flight to search "Mount Mummit". He finds so many mountains of same shape and sizes and ouzo keeps whispering in Shamwill ears that, "we have to go farther" which stresses Shamwill. He comes back with ouzo and discuss the issue with the nobles. Gazualam, King Rim and vizier of Egypt states that, "Don't worry Shamwill, this range is very vast and could be the reason that it will take some time. Just don't be restless and be patient." they begin to rest for the evening. The night falls and Shamwill rests on one of the branches of the tree talking with ouzo. He sees something flying in the sky and in a moment he realizes that it's none other than "Khadinamoon". He recalls and realizes that, he usually visits on every "no moon". He takes his flying carpet with ouzo and follows "Khadinamoon". He finds him leaving towards the sky and he fails to catch his speed. Shamwill resumes flying in the air. While coming down from the air, he finds some cavalry with nobles waiting for him. He lands, all begin to question him, "where have you been with such a speed, we heard a sound of your hurry and came outside of our tents thinking some animals have attacked us". Shamwill replies, "It was not an animal it was our enemy "khadinamoon". He was heading to his sphere. I followed him thinking that he is visiting Amunet but, to my dismay, he already met her and left towards the space." Gazualam consoles Shamwill. King rim replies, "not to worry, with this, it seems that we are close to our goal and Amunet. Let's march tomorrow with all determination, as we are very close."

Gazualam adds, "It's a good sign, now we have to be quick. I think it's the right time to make use of our carpets for patrolling the area". Shamwill nods his head and vizier of Egypt commands, all the army to prepare for further journey.

In Egypt, the king Canopus keeps watching all the activities of the army and nobles with the help of holy priest. He also updates the King Rim's daughter and son-in-law with the events. Therefore, as nobles are aware of the fact that King Canopus have all details and if they face any problem, he is there to provide any help needed. The nobles take flying carpets and get accompanied by each soldier. They go around the range of mountains patrolling the area in search of "Mount Mummit". Shamwill does his surveillance all around but, ouzo keep taking them farther.

Meanwhile, they get down at a point, where Shamwill tells nobles that, "we all know the way to the mountain is from upside, not from below so let ouzo lead us further. As 'Khadinamoon' is very fast with his flight, may be its somewhere around the same range surely. So you all nobles march with army and look for the path with the help of flying carpets, I go farther and keep you informed. I will come back during the evening to update you all about the region." Gazualam replies, "How we will know the way, as ouzo is with you?" Shamwill replies "I have an idea! I will keep on marking the mountains, so that you know the way." King rim appreciates Shamwill's idea and then, Shamwill leaves.

The nobles comes back to army and direct the way as they have been moving forward towards the mountain range. He marks the last mountain where he explores with the help of ouzo. He comes back to the camp with ouzo.

He explains what he has investigated and hence he will rest for the night. The new day arrives for Shamwill, which is loaded with determination and assurance. He takes up flying carpet with ouzo to fly high in search of "Mount Mummit". While flying from morning until evening, he sees ouzo has taken restless flight, much faster than before. The flying carpet is unable to get ouzo in his pace. He flies high and soon abandons Shamwill. Shamwill tries to catch and come close to ouzo disappear in no time. Shamwill look around for ouzo, wherein a point comes that he finds ouzo sitting at the entrance of one of the mountain. The mountain looks very spooky and dark with its elongated stature with the mark of star on it.

Shamwill reaches close to the mountain which has similar signs that were indicated by Amunet. Shamwill just goes energized and excited at what he has found. Ouzo tells

Shamwill that, “this is the huge elevated “Mountain of Mummit” where soul of Amunet is confined and entrance is from here”. Ouzo requests Shamwill that, he should mind his steps forward while walking towards the entrance. All of a sudden Shamwill strides back. He begins taking back his steps, where ouzo flies and sits on his shoulder to inquire the reason for his behaviour. In the interim shamwill sits on flying carpet and surges back towards the nobles.

Shamwill tells ouzo that, "As ‘Khadinamoon’ is the God, so I have to be accompanied by the army as I don’t know what secret fury is added by “Khadinamoon” in this mountain. Shamwill flies back and reveals to all nobles and the army that he had found the “Mount Mummit”. King Rim and Gazualam pays ascribes to the creator for getting them to their destination. The king Canopus continues viewing everything through his enchanted forces about the circumstances. The minute, he hears the declaration by Shamwill about the “Mount Mummit”, he begins to prepare things.

Here Shamwill and all the nobles reach underneath of the “Mount Mummit”. It looks so elevated and vast that they can see only half of it and rest gets covered by fog. Shamwill makes a plan and starts tackling it by himself. He suggest to take flying carpets and fly up to the mountain, at the buckle of entrance. At the entrance, they stop and watch the obnoxious path of Mummit. The entire army begins to converse with each other that, “how elevated thc mountain is? Which, for sure would be deep too, won’t be? Shamwill commands all to stop on the edge and watch out the path, whether if it is has any mystery or danger to it. Army and nobles agree to Shamwill and follow his instructions. Shamwill plans a strategy to test if the entrance is occluded with any mysterious danger. He signals with his head and one of the soldiers gets a flying carpet rolled with a round stone in it. The stone is hurled in the mouth of the mountain.

The stone rolls towards the entrance and they discover mystery pits planned by Khadinamoon for the unwanted guests. Thus, Shamwill makes out and knows now what to be done right away. Shamwill gets on to the flying carpet and tosses another stone while flying with it and he finds the stone falling in a pit making a way. The pit which again joins back to the ground like a lid and finds the entire mouth of the mountain closed with a deadlock cave. He returns and conveys the same to all nobles. In this way all choose to get in to the mountain and begins flying on the carpets.

The carpets carry rolling stones and they toss them in entrance of the cave. With each stone and a flying carpet with various individuals enter the “Mount Mummit”. Shamwill finds the mountain exceptionally dreadful and spooky.

With massive openings, spiked walls and
abnormal sounds of air pressure make the cave look more horrifying. They all enter with ouzo and continue discuss about the unidentified matter, with his master. All of them

follow ouzo who flies with wide golden feathers spread, from a steeply passages of the mountain. They reach at a place where a massive cave opens with enchanting atmosphere.

They discover jelly like ground which is unstable and so shaky (like silicon). All get startled by watching such strange thing on earth. Everybody decides not to land on the ground. While passing from the passages, towards the cave some stones from the walls fall on the ground which are very pointed. The stones are gulped by the jelly ground. All get terrified and begin watching their flying carpet. During reviewing the place, one of the soldier is harmed by a spike of the wall, which is very pointed. He tumbles from the flying carpet and lose his control from it. He falls from the flying carpet towards the jelly ground. He tumbles towards the ground and all of a sudden a huge thunder and light transmitting octopus whose structure is similar to a jelly fish leaves the ground and gulps the entire man in a matter of seconds. All try to save him from the jelly ground wrath, but unfortunately they cannot save him from it.

It's difficult for human to differentiate between the jelly ground and monstrous jelly fish. At the point while flying on a carpet consists of only few soldiers' endeavors to spare him, the octopus discharges electric current with which all get pushed to one corner. All the soldier get frightened and Shamwill commands, "Every one of you, watch your steps as this animal is exceptionally perilous and attacking us, as it is aware of our presence now."

They fly from one corner to the other by keeping themselves away from the jelly ground. By inspecting the place, they finally find a narrow passage which leads inside in more profound end of the mountain. The passage can allow only one person at a time. So they choose to return to the entrance where they can plan a strategy for it. They go back to the entrance and split into groups. They order flying carpets to drop each person one by one. Taking the initiative Shamwill steps up the flying carpet, he flies towards passage and enters in it.

He finds a major mountain excavation followed by a huge cave where the center of the ground is filled with jelly and its creature. The creature encircles all the area so that if anyone comes in contact, it will gulp it all. The moment, others join Shamwill, he continues to inspect the place. The flying carpets continues to pick and drop each one of them from the cavalry. The jelly ground follows all the way from the passage into the cave occupying the central position of the cave surrounded by the dry ground. Shamwill, King and the nobles hears an immense sound of air blowing quickly like a storm from the passage. All takes their positions to prepare for what may be in the store ahead in the menu of surprises, and incredibly now they have to face it. Therefore they see king Canopus entering in jewel Pepins by making the passage broader with his mystical powers.

Shamwill grins at king Canopus as it adds help to him. King Canopus arrives in the cave, and lands on the dry ground where Shamwill and others have positioned themselves. Gazualam asks king Canopus, “How did you find us?” King Canopus replies, "As I told you, through the holy priest and his “future bowl". Shamwill could see all the place comprised of massive cave which has the same serene smell which he witnessed in the valley of “Morah”. He watches all the walls which are very pointed and could even kill if they are not careful about it.

Right off the bat he takes up that it's because of dangerous mountain cave where sure Amunet is confined. However, following to it, he sees above reflecting on the jelly ground, the minute he looks up he witnesses couple of stones floating in the pinnacle of the mountain.

He takes flying carpet and flies high to check. Every one of them tends to watch Shamwill with restlessness. Shamwill flies, ever more higher with much interest. The King Canopus asks, "Is everything alright?" from the ground.

Shamwill informs him from above that “I believe it's a similar stone where Amunet is confined". Shamwill notices couple of stones floating in the air at the pinnacle of the mountain are much bigger in size, than he expected. After watching it more closely he finds one of the stones which is diagonal shaped is emanating light, measuring ten feet tall attached to the pinnacle of the “Mount Mummit.” He feels it like an indication of the same stone mentioned in riddle left by Amunet.

King Canopus orders everybody to take their positions. All the soldiers assemble and encompass the nobles. They all take their positions with raised arches and swords. Shamwill comes down and discusses with the nobles about the further step that can be taken. All disperse and inspect the place carefully. Shamwill brings up to the notice of king Canopus and requests him to rush towards the pinnacle of the mountain. Shamwill and king Canopus gets in jewel Pepins and flies towards the diagonal stone. After reaching closer to it, Shamwill finds Amunet reflections in the stone which is like a crystalline in nature. For a second, he doesn't believe his eyes of what he had found but he becomes cheerful to see the same stone which he was looking for. Amunet goes astounded watching him back. The king Canopus continues watching her without blinking. Shamwill goes closer and touches the stone, something electrifying hurts his hand. King Canopus brings down the jewel Pepin. Shamwill, at the moment, wants to touch, articulate and free Amunet at any cost. The king Rim gives his enchanted bracelet to Shamwill. He asks Shamwill to utilize it close to diagonal stone to remove the curse.

Shamwill and King Canopus fly back and reach to the stone. He utilizes the bracelet to remove the electrifying effect of the stone, which is posing difficulty to touch. With the help of the bracelet the effect gets vanished. Shamwill embraces the stone and reflection of Amunet. She too places her cheeks on the stone wall. King Canopus takes out his lily which was gifted by the world of fairies and smells it, to call Velma. The Velma shows up and solicits that how can she help him. The king asks Velma to free Amunet from the diagonal stone. The Velma answers "If at all I break this crystal stone, you will be having only 60 minutes to unite the body with soul." Shamwill asks then what would be possible at this point. King Canopus questions Velma, “Detach the stone from the mountain so we can carry soul of Amunet with us to unite with the body.” Velma answers "It is impossible, as the stone is the piece of mountain now and disengaging is likewise the same." They start losing hope. They both land down to discuss the matter with king Rim. After arriving down, King Rim presents an idea in front of Shamwill and asks him to continue for his journey. Shamwill gets surprised of what king rim is talking about.

King Rim expounds the thought which he has in his mind. He states to Shamwill that, “Waiting here would bring no help. We can segregate our time by dividing it equally. You keep moving towards the white desert with ouzo and search for the coffin box of Amunet. We will follow you through the holy priest’s “future bowl.” The minute you discover it, we will meet at the gathering point and that time we will get and somehow try to make it possible for all of us. This will save our time and Amunet’s too." Shamwill returns to the stone and conveys to Amunet's soul regarding the process planned by all. Amunet nods her head. Shamwill leaves for further journey.

King Canopus accompanies Shamwill and they fly towards the white desert. They carry everyone on the flying carpet and jewel Pepins and some are left back for the nobles who are present at the “Mount Mummit”. Most of the flying carpets leads towards the white desert with important men and wares. Ouzo guides Shamwill and all head towards the region of Indus. After flying for two days and one night they discover white desert in the eastern side of Indus. Shamwill gets extremely cheerful of finding the place finally. As the desert is very vast they continue to search the exact tempest which leads to Amunet’s body. He comes across storms at significant number of places in the desert. He requests ouzo to direct all towards the right direction. After searching for quite a long time, ouzo finds it. Ouzo leads them more inside the desert. After flying for some time, from there, ouzo signals Shamwill that the tempest which he can see now before him is where Amunet’s coffin is buried. He addresses Shamwill that, “From here you need to hold your breath for 40 minutes to get inside the passage.” Shamwill replies to Ouzo that, “There is no reason for you to worry and I will not come until I get her along with Me.”

In a moment, all reach the place following Shamwill and ouzo alongside to the tempest. They arrive and prepare themselves. They get prepared with their weapons and vital things. King Canopus gives Shamwill a small pot which contains mysterious drops prepared by the holy priest. He suggest him to consume it before hopping into the passage, as it helps humans from breathlessness, in state of unconsciousness, while passing the passage of storm and can reach the place securely. King Canopus prescribes the process of consumption.

Shamwill gets up and prepares to hop inside. This would be the first time though where ouzo would not be accompanying Shamwill. Ouzo makes clamors out of affection, for leaving Shamwill alone. Shamwill embraces ouzo and kisses him, he tells few words of comfort to him on which ouzo agrees. Thus Shamwill leaves towards the passage. Shamwill hops in the passage of tempest. He confronts which takes him somewhere deep inside. Shamwill takes out the pot of drops and consumes the enchanted drops as instructed. He falls oblivious the minute he devours it. Therefore, when he open his eyes he finds himself deep inside the passage.

The passage which is very narrow and difficult even to breathe in. Without realizing anything, he puts his hand in his pocket and discovers dices of the game played by Amunet, which he overlooked during the journey. He kisses them and feels Amunet in it. He gets up and begins to search for the coffin. He finds a massive rock on which a white coffin is placed. He goes restless to reach the place, therefore he rushes towards it. He goes closer and steps up the rock, he opens the coffin where finds a box inside the coffin he opens the box and discovers Amunet's body with no life. He embraces her and kisses her forehead. Tears roll over his cheeks. A thought strikes his mind reminding about Amunet's charm. To avoid army falling for Amunet, he decides to put back the body of Amunet in the coffin and carry it with him covered. The moment he open the coffin the storm resumes outside.

The moment storm resumes, the King, ouzo and the army enter the passage with the help of flying carpets and jewel Pepins. They find Shamwill already standing ready with the coffin. They carry Shamwill and the coffin through the passage. All come out from the passage with the feeling of achievement but Shamwill is still worried.

Chapter Twenty

The Moving Himalayas (Indus Kingdom)

On the other hand, with the help of holy priest king Rim and Gazualam get all the information related to coffin and wait for Shamwill to reach at the gathering point. Ouzo guides Shamwill towards the meeting point. He leads all towards the northern part of Indus in a vast mountain range. It has freezing temperature and all the nobles and the army begin to shiver. They warm up themselves with the same flying carpets every here and there and continue to proceed with their journey.

After flying for long time ouzo whispers in Shamwill's ear that, “. He tells "my master the very next is the mountain which are looking for.” Shamwill commands everybody, to stop at the next pinnacle of the mountain as right underneath is the mountain they were searching for.

He looks at the sky and notices something and therefore adds, “It’s the perfectly right mountain which is just beneath to the red star which is none other than star “Rigel”. Ouzo assets that, “this is the right and highest pinnacle of the mountain, from the range of mountains called “Himalayas”. They watch unbelievable occurrence underneath their flying carpets. They witness the range of mountains moving in the shape of a star which is a process designed by “Khadinamoon” to watch the movement of mountains from “Rigel” intending that Amunet is still encaged and if the mountain stops moving, which has a system to bring up to the notice of him, if anyone disturbs its normal behaviour.

Ouzo whispers that, “we need to stay in the air in suspended motion until the moment, the soul of Amunet is brought here.” Shamwill and King Canopus figures out to get Amunet. They come up to a conclusion that they attempts would consume a lot of time and they need to hurry up as the process lacks time.

King Canopus chooses to use his lily. Velma shows up, King Canopus orders Velma to carry the diagonal stone with his left over army before 60 minutes from the minute of extrication.

Velma guarantees that it would take her 10 minutes to accomplish the task. Shamwill grins out of such quick administration.

Subsequently, Velma vanishes, Shamwill plans about the further process. Ouzo answers, "Amunet’s body must be placed over the diagonal stone and after that it she will come to life, however the minute stone is extricated from the mountain, ‘Khadinamoon’ comes to know about it. Also, beyond any doubt he will surge towards earth." Shamwill falls in deep thoughts where king Canopus requests Shamwill to be patient. In a while Velma shows up with the stone and the remaining army near Mount Mummit.

It's a very big turning point for Shamwill as he can touch, feel and smell Amunet. Furthermore, in addition to it, her impression of soul in a diagonal stone makes him feel so invigorated. He can't envision his eagerness would allow him to see Amunet alive before him. It's the priceless moment for him, for which he is ready to conquer the whole world.

Shamwill welcomes and meets everyone. As they are in air on flying carpets and on jewel Pepins, its little painstaking for all to embrace each other as per their cultures.

Chapter Twenty One

Reunion of Soul & Body

Eventually, Shamwill surges towards the stone had by Velma. As instructed by ouzo, Shamwill takes up the coffin and takes out the body of Amunet. Watching stunning body of Amunet all get lost. Conceived in a human race, all people are infatuated towards Amunet's attractive appearance. Their eyes get wide open along with their mouths. Her appeal makes everybody feel enchanted to her.

As Shamwill knows how he was lost in Amunet's charm he chooses to first follow the process of getting her back to life and later secure her as well. Shamwill places the body on the diagonal stone. As Amunet's soul is a goddess soul it has multiple colours like rainbow in it. The "Himalayan" mountains which were moving stop at their last positions. Ouzo flies above to the Amunet's body and penetrates red rays from his eyes on the diagonal stone which squashes the stone into pieces.

The stone cracks and soul of Amunet which is in cool lime shade comes out and enters the body. Amunet is lifted noticeably to all and after the soul enters the body, she drops from the air. Shamwill holds her body on the flying carpet and embraces her. Amunet still stays unconscious and Shamwill turns up his head in bliss to share his happiness, to his surprise he sees everybody lost in Amunet's charm.

Taking her in his arms he continues to feel her. In a while all hear a big thunder roaring from the sky. The star Rigel begins to emit red light like a ruby. Shamwill and everyone get occupied watching the disaster. Each one of them watches the sky and ouzo advises to Shamwill that, "Khadinamoon has come to know about Amunet. Now, how to save her from him. He will come to you in no time." King Rim reminds Shamwill about the bracelet. Shamwill nods his head.

King Rim recommends Shamwill to take away Amunet in the mystery world of bracelet as soon as he can. Where "Khadinamoon" can never enter. Shamwill considers the plan to be extremely persuading. In a minute, Amunet comes back to her consciousness. Amunet gets up and begins to grin at Shamwill. With a beautiful smile, she embraces him firmly. Amunet tells Shamwill with tears in her eyes that, "I have never expected that you would put yourself in such a big peril for me and never knew that you will make it."

Also, along these lines the shade of her eyes changes. Shamwill says, "I love you Amunet and cannot change this truth." Listening to it tears rolls out from her eyes. All hear blasting sound. The moment they turn up to see, they discover fire balls falling from the Star Rigel towards the earth on "Himalayas". All rush to leave the place and

Shamwill tells Amunet that, "I am sending you to the most secure place and very soon i will come to see you."

He opens up the sleeve and tosses the light from the bracelet and requests Amunet to enter in the iced wall. Amunet embraces Shamwill and enters in the wall. She vanishes in a matter of seconds. Shamwill rushes to wind up and step on his flying carpet. Escaping the fire balls all surge to step on flying carpets.

The fire balls are just about to fall on the area where Amunet has been brought back to life, where, very moment Shamwill escapes from the fire balls on his flying carpet. The fire balls start raining on all places over the earth. Anyway they have a flying tools to escape and all rush towards Egypt. After passing from the mountain ranges, oceans, valleys and various kingdoms. All reach the Kingdom of Egypt and fly towards the king's castle. After landing on the royal palace of the king, they take a sigh of relief unknowing the fact that fire balls are being fired all over the earth. Shamwill decides to rest as he is exceptionally tired of his long exhausting journey.

After resting for some time, Shamwill hurries to see his mother. Gazualam accompanies Shamwill to the caves on their unicorns. Mother Amyra gets so happy after watching Shamwill and Gazualam. She gets some information about the journey and hugs Shamwill. Her eyes goes numb. Shamwill narrates whole the journey. After listening to everything mother Amyra asks Shamwill as to where

Amunet is. Shamwill opens up his sleeve and takes mother to the Amunet.

After entering the mystery world of bracelet, Amyra gets stunned. He takes the mother to Amunet. Amunet gets so upbeat after watching Shamwill and his mother. Mother Amyra assures Amunet and tells her to hold on for some more days in the world of bracelet. On a personal note Amyra says to Shamwill that she is very beautiful with every appeal of a Goddess and have never witnessed such a charm on any women in her lifetime. Amunet agrees and chooses to wait until the battle. Shamwill consoles her and leaves with the mother Amyra from the world of bracelet.

Over the earth they discover fire balls being hurled at people and their kingdoms, so they move people to the caves of the mountains taking them away from the cities. King Rim sends his commander-in-chief to his city and asks to rescue, with all measures, to defend his people. King Rim again, meets his daughter Celin and son-in-law Olax and uncovers the entire fiasco. The son-in-law Olax is to return to the world of mermaids and discloses about the wrath that the world is presently confronting.

King Rim and Celin let Prince Olax leave momentarily towards the mermaid kingdom to fulfill his duties. The King Canopus still can't trust his eyes, the beauty of Amunet makes him loose his senses for some time. He continues to praise her everywhere regardless, of minding any place. After coming outside from the mystery world, mother

Amyra wants to thank every individual who helped her son in this difficult and mysterious mission.

In between these circumstances, vizier of Egypt beseeches Shamwill and intimates him about the meeting at the court. Mother Amyra feels that she can thank everybody in the meantime at the table of discussion. She insists Shamwill to take her to the court to thank everyone for his mission. Shamwill, Mother Amyra and Gazualam heads towards the court where King Rim, King Canopus and other nobles are waiting for them to find the solution for “Khadinamoon”. The moment Amyra joins the table, she gets surprised to discover King Rim in the court.

King Rim couldn't trust his eyes at what he is watching before him. Mother Amyra gets stagger and shakes with no reason. Shamwill asks his mother for the reason of such conduct. King Rim states, "Queen Amyra, is that you? Are you alive?" Shamwill replies, "Yes she disclosed to me that she is a queen, but how do you know her?" King rim answers out of tremendous happiness, "She is my better half". Mother Amyra goes dumbfounded and breaks down. King Rim approaches them with falling steps. He states, "I am very glad to see you alive and furthermore compliment you for your marriage with Gazualam and brave son Shamwill." Gazualam asserts, "Dear King it is not the truth. She isn't my significant other and still holds the position of a queen and your better half indeed." King rim goes dumbfounded. He asks, "Then Shamwill?" Gazualam replies, “She was pregnant when left the kingdom and Shamwill is none other than, “your son and future of

Kingdom Cyrene." It is a big astonishment for all at the king's court. Shamwill just watches king rim without blinking, as he invested such an incredible time with him, without realizing that he is his biological father. King Rim comes forward and embraces Shamwill out of love but, mother Amyra gets resentful that king Rim considered her dead.

Shamwill and Gazualam support her and request her to forgo past and move ahead with acceptance. All take their seat at the table to take out a solution for "khadsinamoon" and fury that he discharged on earth. Vizier of Egypt keeps the statistical data points before all that fire is burning all parts of the world and if not ceased, it could eradicate life on the planet.

One of the messengers during the discussion informs Gazualam that the six sons of him are convicted in a neighbouring country of Cyrene for stealing diamonds. Listening to it Gazualam chooses to put the matter aside until the war.

Shamwill approaches the King Canopus for all arrangements of the war. King Rim instructs to take guidance with respect and discussion with couple of Gods. A messenger is sent to king of Persia looking for assistance from God of Water. All disperse from the lobby. Now, mother Amyra does not have to conceal anything because she is still a better half of the King Rim. After watching mother Amyra and only brother Shamwill, Celin breaks into tears. The reunion of a family makes everybody cheerful and a strong will of getting back his love adds stars to Shamwill's happiness.

But, this satisfaction does not stay for long time. The fire balls continue to burn the kingdoms and villages. The king of Persia joins at the King's table. All Kings request the help from the Persian King to seek assistance from God of Water. To tackle this terrible situation, king of Persia agrees and supplicates with his priest seeking help from the God of water. The God shows up and Shamwill puts forward this critical situation.

The God of Water agrees to help Shamwill and in the same manner he chooses to bring the matter to the notice of God of climate (God Adlam) who is none other than father of Amunet. The God of water approaches the God Adlam (God of Climate) and unveils the issue of Amunet. The God Adlam goes frantic out of bliss for his daughter's update. He decides to meet Shamwill instantly. He flies down earth to Egypt to see Shamwill and soon after meeting him, he decides to be a part of the battle and rebuff khadinamoon.

Shamwill takes the God Adlam to mystery world of bracelet and reunites father & daughter. God Adlam insists Amunet to stay in the mystery world until the war for her safety. Amunet cries so much that anyone might have cried watching her in return. It's the greatest moment for her, as it has been years that she didn't meet any of her family. The King Adlam (God of Climate) changes the climate pattern in such a way that all fire balls swing back to the star Rigel. "Khadinamoon" gets furious and stops firing at the earth. “Khadinamoon” assembles up for a conference with all Gods and God of Climate to know the sudden change in atmosphere. Where God of water who is aware of everything is also a part of it.

In a gathering at the court of heaven, “Khadinamoon” demands the destruction of entire mankind where all divine beings reject his will and wish. God Adlam discloses to everyone about “Khadinamoon” and the misfortune that he made to Aabr and to the goddess Amunet. After hearing it, all Gods support God Adlam and conflicts with “Khadinamoon”. Khadinamoon states, "When I was on Rigel, Amunet was rescued by a human and now I demand Amunet with Aabr." Consequently, Khadinamoon goes against all divine beings, in result, pronouncing a war against all Gods and humans of earth.

The God of Water and God of Climate (King Adlam) shows up and reveals it to all that “Khadinamoon” has demanded a war. They order everyone to get ready for the war and protect Amunet with each basic help. The battle between good and evil. For saving earth and its mankind is going to begin, where it never happened that all Gods and human race stood against one God of element, who turned out to be a greedy beast.

Chapter Twenty Two

The Second Day of the Battle field

The divine force who created all is watching everything as he does always. For the creator everything is only a play area and who whenever plays, he wins. Now the game plans are made for a phenomenal and uncommon war. What's more, let's remember of what occurred on the first day of battle in the beginning.

Now, Amyra takes a gander at the sovereign Hashlam and she finds him asleep. Mother Amyra approaches Shamwill to check whether he is in sound sleep so that he wakes up fresh on the following day to battle. She watches him at comfort and therefore she leaves to rest in her chamber for the next day.

Next day of battle (second day)

The following day has appeared again with its challenges for Shamwill. It is by all accounts, the final day of the war. However, Shamwill has recovered from his wounds and is in better condition. Now, he is in a state to fight.

Every one of the king vows to begin the fight and desires to have triumph at any cost.

The King Canopus is in extreme anger puts his hand under in one of his pockets of his royal outfit and takes out a pouch studded with emeralds and begins to open its rope. He takes out enchanted sand and blow it all around the battle field. Each of the mountains starts evolving in the battlefield and begins to transform into mammoth fire emitting horses. Watching it "Khadinamoon" gets surprised and raises his eyebrow. He realizes that human of earth are also difficult to defeat and have been bestowed by supernatural powers too.

After transforming into the beast, "Khadinamoon" gets irate and takes out his hands which changes into brutal weapon. He keeps running towards the army and lift them to shred them apart. Shamwill just can't wait and sends his another regiment of soldiers accompanied by divine creatures to attack him. The Soldiers, Amoos and Burq begins to attack the opposite side. They spit acids and transform the creatures of regel into skeletons. "Khadinamoon" begins losing his patience after watching consecutive counterblast from the opponent. All the divine beings sit down in the sky. They begin to destroy "Khadinamoon" army with their various powers.

After utilizing all of his otherworldly powers in the battlefield, "Khadinamoon" chooses to be his best in wicked back up plan. He transforms up into lethal brute/creature which is extremely huge in size. Watching him in this incarnation all get terrified as they have never witnessed such creature. Shamwill raises his eyebrow and jumps in the battle field to fight with "khadinamoon". Shamwill bounces on his unicorn and heads towards "khadinamoon" with his army.

An extraordinary and unusual battle takes place between immortal and mortal where being human Shamwill wins over Khadinamoon. He escapes from the paws of him with his best in Tahtib and other skills. Shamwill hurts Khadinamoon at couple of pivotal parts including his wings, back and knee. The mother Amyra and the general population from entire world continues supplicating strongly. Watching petitions and prayers of people and Shamwill's determination in battle against abhorrent, and to safeguard his love, the creator comes into action.

The creator sends couple of high positioned heavenly angels with a pine box to battle field. The heavenly angels have astonishing plumes which are huge and their eyes illuminating spark. The heavenly angels carry a golden cage with them. Viewing those heavenly angels Khadinamoon screams out of fear, "No, you can't do this to me creator. You gave me boon and now cannot take from me back. Amunet is all mine and I am the king of climate."

The angels sent by the creator walk toward Khadinamoon and extract his soul and pushes his callous body in a pine box. His soul is confined in a cage which they got from paradise. They take away Khadinamoon from the battle field. As Khadinamoon is a God of fire, he can't be destructed on earth and possibly the creator has second thoughts for him. All monster Sherries of Rigel flare up with unusual shrieks back to their homeland from the battle ground.

The battlefield is calm and quiet with only human presence. With great victory heard in silence. Everybody praises the bargain and the triumph of good over evil. Amunet returns from the mystery world of bracelet with lots of joy. Each of them, makes merry with celebration and mirth. The King rim takes Shamwill and Queen Amyra with all due respect back from the battlefield. It's a moment of pride for the King Canopus. Celebration with big crackers and all starts their journey towards Egypt in flying carpets and jewel Pepin's. The performers light the sky with fire crackers and various types of flying performances.

Chapter Twenty Three

The Wedding

King Rim finds Gazualam stressed and weak. By overlooking the worries of Gazualam, the King Rim takes up his voyage to Cyrene. After coming to the city, the people appreciate and celebrates out of happiness for the victory achieved by Shamwill. It's an honorable moment for king rim and Shamwill. King Rim honours Shamwill with the position of "The King" and should be crowned after him, from where Shamwill would be the King of Cyrene. The sister Celin is very happy and content with the arrival of mother and brother.

King Rim announces the wedding ceremony of Shamwill with Amunet in the grand country of Cyrene. After declaration, the God Adlam takes Amunet back to Aabr. Amunet bliss with joy and happiness. Before leaving for Aabr King Rim and God Adlam starts discussing about the wedding dates. God Adlam gives consent to wed Amunet with Shamwill on the following "full moon" which is by all accounts following after 20 to 25 days from the present date. King rim likewise agrees to the matter. Amunet leaves Ouzo to Shamwill with the intension that, if any message can be passed on by ouzo to Aabr by Shamwill.

God Adlam is very happy that at last Shamwill has defeated a monstrous wicked god and saved the world from a big destruction. He is glad that he has found a human with golden heart for his girl, who is likewise from a bloodline of king. Amunet being so shy thinking about her wedding blushes in adoration for Shamwill. All carry pre wedding arrangements at Aabr.

The day passes by and Shamwill lives the life which he never imagined. He carries on with his life of a Prince with his royal family but, he continues to miss Gazualam in each aspect of life. After long restlessness, he sends a messenger to get Gazualam. The minute Gazualam hears the message that Shamwill is missing him, he travels back with the messenger to see Shamwill. Gazualam takes up voyage to a distance with their recollections and memories. He reaches to the City Cyrene, the minute Shamwill sees Gazualam entering his palace, he embraces him and kisses him on his forehead. Both begin to cry with tears and warmth in their eyes.

Gazualam asks Shamwill, "How are you? It's been long that I have seen you." Shamwill answers I know father even I miss your presence each minute." Gazualam continues grinning and watching Shamwill whole heartedly. Shamwill includes "I am honoured that I have been raised under you. I have so many things to discuss with you, however first how about we eat something now?" Gazualam gestures his head and takes a bliss. They sit to have it and continue to discuss things occurring around them.

The King Rim comes to know about the visit of Gazualam and he leaves everything to attend him. He joins Shamwill and Gazualam with lots of joy. He embraces him and request him to take his seat. Shamwill takes consent from Gazualam and King Rim to join them back soon as he has some issues to wind up on priority basis. The king Rim and Gazualam continues to converse. Gazualam shares his worry with the king. King Rim gets fretful, as he disregarded the issue of "Egress Empyrean" of Bamiyan Mountains. The countenance turns pale. They continue to discuss. The attendant presents refreshments before the royals.

The Queen Amyra is informed about the visit of Gazualam to the palace, she comes to see Gazualam, leaving her priorities. While walking towards the grand corridor, she finds both worried with some issue, she sees through a window of the corridor. Watching queen, Gazualam signals King Rim. Both stand and welcome her in honour. Queen Amyra requests Gazualam not to stand for her as she owes so much to him. She sees their appearances full of anxiety.

At that point, both act as if they were discussing about some random issues associated to kingdom and they preclude from claiming any reason. Queen Amyra continues watching their pale countenances (facial expression) for long time, she tries to find out the reason which they are trying to conceal from her. King Rim requests Gazualam to stay back with him at least until the wedding ceremony. Gazualam agrees and stays back in the royal residence of the King.

Continuously, queen finds both discussing deeply about something with lot of interest and when questioned to them, they deny of anything as such. The interest grows more for the queen to find out the reason behind their discussion. The time comes when there are just three days left for the marriage, where all guests assemble to attend the pre wedding celebrations before the main wedding. The guests include Gods, King of Persia, King Canopus, Saints and neighborhood Kingdoms.

Shamwill sees that King Rim and Gazualam are in distress and their faces are going dull in sadness. Queen Amyra asks Shamwill to find out the reason behind their condition. Shamwill watches them with such an extensive amount of intrigue. Shamwill answers "I see them in so much worry". Queen also affirms that she likewise feels the same since long she is watching them conversing. Shamwill and queen decide to approach them and ask about the reason for their worry.

Gazualam requests not to question anything about their concerns, but Shamwill does not allow him. He request him so much that at last he concedes. Queen Amyra asks Gazualam the reason for his concerns. He replies that, "In the third month of Shamwill marriage, Shamwill will die as he is carrying a bane of which he was unaware of." Queen Amyra loses her senses and tumble down. Shamwill holds his mother and questions Gazualam, “Are you joking? What made you say that father? Is that by any reason you don’t like Amunet?" The king Rim asserts, “It’s the truth and simply don't ask anything further, as we don't have any solution to it.” It is a big shock for Shamwill. He states "How it happened and why am I not aware of it?”

He insists all to tell the truth. Watching his pleas they decide to reveal it to Shamwill. King Rim and Gazualam narrate the entire story of Bamiyan Mountains, Listening to it Shamwill falls and gives up his hope. King Rim and Gazualam binds Shamwill in a promise that this should not to be disclosed to anyone as it would result in destruction for the whole Egypt. Shamwill sends Ouzo to arrange a meeting with Amunet. Amunet accompanies her parents to meet Shamwill. Shamwill tells Amunet that he can't wed her and if he does, then he will die third month from the wedding date.

Amunet answers "I think you are kidding with me before the marriage? Is that any reason that you would prefer not to wed me? Did I hurt you? Are your parents against it?" Amunet just can't accept what Shamwill just told her. Amunet loves Shamwill deeply and that is why she is not able to handle this reality. Shamwill says he too loves her from the bottom of his heart and can do anything for her happiness and neglects the future occurrence.

Amunet states to Shamwill that, "I can't live without you and can’t accept what you are disclosing to me." Even the parents of Amunet accuse Shamwill of double crossing and abandoning their daughter for other women. To prove his affection and love he is compelled to wed Amunet.

The day which was chosen had not changed. The ceremony begins and the entire Cyrene city is enlivened with lights and blooms. The Mother Amyra takes up the charge for her son’s marriage. Amunet comes in her best dress with all precious diamonds studded body with light emanating appeal and marvelous divine charm added to her eyes. With everything she ever wanted, for her marriage and a sun kissed face where happiness is spouting out.

What's more, Shamwill was also prepared with his extravagant clothing and attractive looks leaves everybody staggered. This is the most anticipated and desired day for Shamwill and Amunet. Shamwill and everyone lose all sense of direction in the appeal of Amunet. Goddess Hassha recites a spell on people so that they don't fall in Amunet's charm. Keeping witness to the entire world and Gods the couple get proclaimed as husband and wife. Amunet and Shamwill thanks everyone wholeheartedly.

Despite being a human and a Godless, no limits can prevent Amunet and Shamwill from getting to be one. Both get to know one another. For couple of weeks they overlook the entire world. Amunet flies high with her wings and Shamwill gives wings to her desires. Shamwill flies in his flying carpet high in the sky with Amunet cherishing the moments of his life. Shamwill continues contemplating the revile he is carrying with him, yet love of Amunet keeps his mind diverted. In the middle of those brilliant moments Amunet confirms that she is pregnant and bearing a child of Shamwill. Shamwill couldn't simply hold his happiness and runs frantic out of affection with her. He states that, "It will be the first race on earth who would be uncommon blend of human and goddess". It turns into a defining moment for Queen Amyra, King Rim and Gazualam to have such elegant period after such a hard time.

Chapter Twenty Four

The Strange Last Wish

What's more, it happens to be the third month that Shamwill begins hacking and in couple of minutes his body turns cold. Amunet and Queen Amyra rushes to see him. All take him to the bed of royal room and call the holy priest of Cyrene. The priest pronounces him dead. Amunet cries inconsolably for not trusting him and disregarding his admonitions. She embraces Shamwill firmly and cries out loud. All the castle and attendants assemble to see the issue, but nobody can help Shamwill.

King Rim and Gazualam know about the reality. They realize that they couldn't help Shamwill on it. Amunet cries out loud and kisses Shamwill allover. During sobbing, Amunet finds a letter in Shamwill's pocket. She opens and reads it.

It reveals that "My Love Amunet, I know you didn't trust me however now you will. I loved you always and will be yours until eternity. Give my love to my father Gazualam, my other father King Rim, and my mother Amyra and sister Celin. My heaps of adoration to my "part" who will bc coming soon in this world. I could never return however my love will always be with you forever. Expressing my last wish that my coffin should be placed in thc cavc of Debuck caves situated in the Egypt. Ensure nobody returns for it. My final goodbyes..." Amunet cries unlimitedly and asks the secret behind it. But as it's too late for her, Shamwill's body docs not react. Amunet gets furious due to the mystery behind the demise of Shamwill and the shade of her eyes changes. Mother Amyra reconsoles Amunet and sympathizes with her.

For the last rites and entombment they leave for Egypt. In transit the entire kingdom observes mourning in distress and torment.

Numerous warriors discuss Shamwill and his heroics. Amunet continues craving for Shamwill by sitting close to his body. Mother Amyra who is seated in the chariot cries aloud consistently for Shamwill. King Rim consoles Amunet and Queen Amyra. They enter Egypt, the city is turned into black colour in Shamwill's respect.

They reach Egypt and entombment rituals start. King Rim is in grief about his son. He had just given farewell whom he met after such a long time. He could not withstand due to sorrow and kept on taking deep sighs. Queen Amyra just can't hold her tears and she chooses to remain quiet. Gazualam Nergal has raised Shamwill with so much of affection and this incident has made him stunned as well. He continues recalling the time spent with Shamwill.

All the knowledge he provided to him continuously (teachings with love) torments his brain in sadness. Everybody conveys sympathies to the families of Shamwill and Amunet. God Adlam comes to the passing away of Shamwill, unable to control his feelings he goes numb while offering sympathies and expresses his statements of regret to mother Amyra for not trusting Shamwill. They demand Amunet to join them, but Amunet requests to the father that, "I would prefer to be on earth for some time".

After paying homage, sympathies and condolences God Adlam and Goddess Hassha leave with sadness. According to Shamwill's will his body should be kept in a cave and nobody visit him afterwards. They leave Shamwill's body in coffin as instructed. Amunet embraces Shamwill's body and sheds tears in his memory. Mother Amyra pats Amunet's back and demands her to leave from the place with them.

The Last Chapter

The Clue of the Coffin

Amunet being goddess in her own persona, she sense things to be unexplainable. Her inclination which is not as same as others feels herself as a devotee of Shamwill. She wants to end her life also but a thought of their coming child prevents her from doing it.

She wipes her tears and raises her brows. King Rim, King Canopus and others call everybody to the royal palace with lot of grief. After reaching the royal palace in sadness, Queen Amyra feels awful for Amunet. She tells everybody that, "Being a mother I feel so much pain and I sorry for Amunet for such a short wedded relationship." She turns back and desires to see Amunet, thinking she is walking behind her but to her surprise she finds is Amunet missing. She sends troops around to search for her but no one finds Amunet. The very moment the incident is brought up to the notice of Kings and the other nobles. All get worried and surge back to the cave and shockingly they neither discover the coffin nor Amunet.

All go astounded about the secret behind the incident of Shamwill and Amunet. Two days pass by searching for them and still nobody discovers anything. King Canopus asks the holy priest to check the status of Amunet. The holy priest checks in his magical bowl and amazingly he finds Amunet alive. He sees that she is perched on a branch of a tree. What is more shocking is that she is happy and glad about something. All get astonished with the circumstance. King Rim requests that the priests to check the surroundings so they can find the place and rescue her.

The holy priest says it's the most perilous place where no human is permitted to enter and I am dazed that how Amunet went there in such a brief timeframe. All look stunned towards one other. The King Rim answers "May be because she is a goddess!" The most amazing part begins when the priest discovers coffin of Shamwill very next to Amunet with no body in it. Rest to be continued.

FIND YOUR PUZZLE

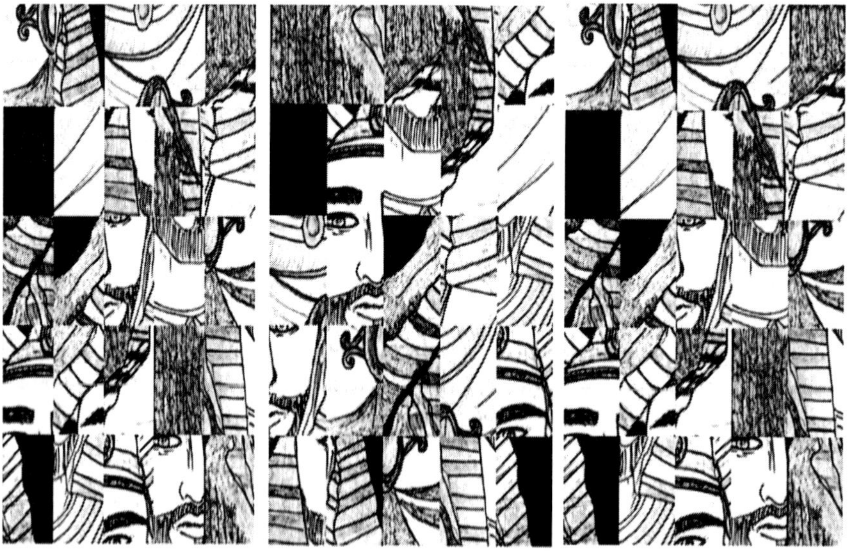

Notes